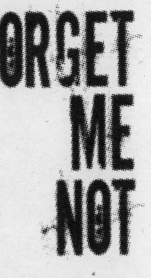

FORGET ME NOT

Where was Mum?

Lightning cracked at the edge of my vision. At the same time the children along the way squealed and shouted. The sky was darkening and the air was like a hot fog.

Something would happen.

That's what it felt like. I thought it would be the rain, the storm. I wasn't ready for anything else.

Other books by Anne Cassidy

FORGET ME NOT

anne cassidy

SCHOLASTIC

First published in the UK in 2008 by Scholastic Children's Books
An imprint of Scholastic Ltd
Euston House, 24 Eversholt Street
London, NW1 1DB, UK
Registered office: Westfield Road, Southam, Warwickshire, CV47 0RA
SCHOLASTIC and associated logos are trademarks and or registered
trademarks of Scholastic Inc.

10 digit ISBN 0 439 94290 X
13 digit ISBN 978 0439 94290 4

British Library Cataloguing-in-Publication Data.
A CIP catalogue record for this book
is available from the British Library

Printed by CPI Bookmarque, Croydon, Surrey
Papers used by Scholastic Children's Books are made from wood grown
in sustainable forests.

1 3 5 7 9 10 8 6 4 2

www.scholastic.co.uk/zone

PROLOGUE

A small child weighs a tiny amount. I know this.

This child was lying on her back. She was hot I could tell. When I bent down I could feel the heat emanating from her, I could smell it.

I stopped for a moment, thinking I'd heard something from far away in the trees. A dangerous sound. But it was just some animal crying out, scuttling away through the undergrowth. I pulled myself together and stared at her for a long time. I was hardly breathing. I didn't want to make a sound in case I woke anyone up.

I held my hands in a square as if to frame a picture.

She was a beauty.

I reached down, careful not to wake her. My hands slid under her and I lifted her up, pulling her into my chest. She murmured something in her sleep and I closed my eyes with sheer pleasure.

Then I took her away.

ONE

Epping

All evening it felt like something was going to happen. At nine it was still hot, the air thick and warm as soup. Every time I went out into the garden there were big soft drops of rain that dotted the paving stones for a few seconds then dried up. The sky was baggy and there were random claps of thunder that made me jump every time I heard them.

I'd spent hours sorting my old school stuff out, my files and books. My last exam had finished the previous week and I wanted to get rid of everything. School was over and I wanted to put it far behind me. I hooked out my diary, which had been in the bottom of my bag, hardly ever used.

Kimble High School Stella Parfitt Form 12c

Twelve years of education. Stella Parfitt, school student, was no more. In her place was a new person. Someone who would have a job, an income, a tax number, a proper bank account and a credit card. I wanted to leave learning and books and exams behind. I was changing, finally closing the door on smelly schools and exasperated teachers.

I dragged another black bag full of notes through the

3

kitchen. I shoved the back door open with my foot and felt the warm air roll over me. I dumped the bag by the bin and stood still for a moment. I could almost *hear* the heat humming gently around me. I pulled the front of my blouse out and fanned my midriff.

Thunder cracked in the night sky. I looked up for lightning but couldn't see it. Beyond the gardens, in the forest, I could hear kids playing, screaming at the tops of their voices. And the sound of motorbikes riding along the bridle paths. For a moment I wished I was out there with them, on the back of a bike, tearing up and down the forest, feeling the air rush past me.

I pulled a chair out of the kitchen on to the patio and sat on it with a glass of iced water. After drinking I held the glass up to my cheek. It would be another night of damp sheets and open windows. And where was Mum? *I'm popping out*, she'd said, after tea, and I hadn't seen her since. I stared at the wall of trees along the bottom of my garden. Why hadn't she called? I sighed. I undid the buttons of my blouse and flapped the material to cool down. It felt good so I left it hanging open.

Where was she?

Lightning cracked at the edge of my vision. At the same time the children along the way squealed and shouted. The sky was darkening and the air was like a hot fog.

Something would happen.

That's what it felt like. I thought it would be the rain, the storm. I wasn't ready for anything else.

*

4

About eleven I found the letter about my mum's job interview. I was looking for a magazine in her bedroom. On her desk, next to her computer, was a piece of headed notepaper. *Dear Teresa Parfitt*, it said, *Reference your application for the post of Senior Administrator. You have been shortlisted for this post and we would be pleased if you could attend an interview on July 9th at 10.00 a.m. Hotel and travel expenses will be reimbursed.*

My mum had mentioned applying for new jobs. What she hadn't said was that the job was in Liverpool. We lived in Essex. I put the letter down and walked away. I returned a moment later, sat down in the desk chair and picked it up again. Liverpool?

What was Mum thinking? We were happy living here. We knew lots of people. We got on well with our neighbours and Mum had lots of friends.

The sound of rain hitting the window made me look up. I walked across and pulled the net curtain aside. I expected to see a deluge but there was only some spots on the glass, nothing in the air outside. No rain, no breeze, no cool air, just suffocating heat. A ragged flash of lightning lit up the sky for a second and I could see the tops of the trees in the forest. Then it was dark again. My shoulders felt tight and I looked at the clock. It was eleven twenty. Where is Mum? I thought, looking back at the letter, lying ominously on her desk. Thunder mumbled in the distance as I went back into my room and picked my mobile up and moved the cursor until I had the word *Mum* on the screen. I pressed the call button and listened to the ring tone until the voicemail came on.

Why should I be surprised that she hadn't told me about Liverpool? She was good at keeping secrets. Birthdays and Christmases were no problem for her. She hid things skilfully.

A siren sounded in the distance. Probably a fire engine. There'd been lots of them in the past few days, screaming up the road heading for the forest and the fires that had been breaking out all over the place.

I went into my room and clicked on the fan. It started to move in a slow semicircle, riffling the clothes that were hanging on the back of my chair and making ripples on my sheets. I turned the lamp off, got undressed and put my nightie on. Before getting into bed I stood by the window looking out. I could see the line of gardens below. There were a few voices from neighbouring houses and the sound of the dog from next door but one barking.

Beyond the gardens the forest lay silent. A great dark mass that seemed exhausted by the heat. I looked into it for any sign of life. There was nothing. My eye flicked from right to left and back again, searching for the light that sometimes shone up from the headlights of a car as it drove through. Nothing.

Where was Mum?

I was tense. Waiting for her. Waiting for the rain. Waiting for something to happen.

The rain came about two. It hit the window like a shower of pebbles. It woke me up and I stumbled out of bed to close it and watched as it fell in a sheet of water past the glass. It felt chilly and I rubbed my arms. The sound of the front door closing made me look round.

"Mum?" I called.

I went out on to the landing and turned the light on. My mum was drenched. Her hair was flat and her clothes were soaked.

"Are you all right? Where have you been?" I said, going down the stairs.

"Oh Stel," she said, her voice slurred, "I'm all right. I got a bit wet. . ."

"You're soaked!" I said. "Come upstairs and get these wet things off!"

"I need a drink of water," she said.

I followed her into the kitchen. At the sink she kicked her shoes off and held a glass under the tap. She drank some and then refilled it. The rain was skimming across the kitchen window, blurring the darkness. Mum turned to me, smaller now in her bare feet. She was drunk. I suddenly knew where she'd been.

"You didn't go round to see Gerry Boyd!"

"Don't start, Stel," she said, walking past me.

I walked after her. I could smell the alcohol off her. She paused a couple of times on the stairs and I stood behind her, my hand out in case she lost her footing. In the bedroom she put the light on and left the glass on the edge of her bedside table. When she started to peel her clothes off I stepped across and pulled the curtains shut. She was standing in her bra and pants.

"Just need to go to the toilet," she said.

7

"You've been to Gerry Boyd's, haven't you?" I said.

She didn't answer. Her skin looked washed out under the light. She walked past me out to the bathroom. The only bright thing about her was the blue flower tattoo on her shoulder.

Why wouldn't she just say where she'd been?

"I need to go to bed," she said, giving me a kiss on the cheek. "Can't be late for work tomorrow. Got a meeting."

She lay on the bed in her underwear, her face pushed into the pillow. She wasn't like someone's mum. She was a like naughty teenager. I pulled the sheet up over her and clicked the light off. All I could hear was the rain falling, softer now, like water in a passing stream.

She'd been with Gerry Boyd, I was sure. She hadn't told me she was going to see him. She'd kept it a secret. She was good at that.

TWO

The bad news spread slowly. Police cars that were parked outside the Hendersons' alerted a few early risers. I eventually heard about it from neighbours.

I was in the kitchen, making some breakfast. The back door and windows were open to let the fresh air into the house. The rain had stopped but everywhere was damp. The grass and shrubs were reaching up, glistening with moisture. After days of looking dusty and brown, the garden was a loud green.

It was just gone seven-thirty and I was thinking about Liverpool. Why had Mum applied for a job so far away?

I thought of Gerry Boyd, Mum's on/off boyfriend. I tapped my fingers on the kitchen table, my teeth knocking against each other. I pictured him sitting on Mum's bed, in the middle of the night, a few weeks before. He'd been strumming his guitar, his legs crossed, his feet in big leather sandals. Mum had been dancing around the room, a glass of red wine in her hand. *Oops*, she'd said when she saw me standing there. *Did we wake you up?*

Now Gerry was seeing someone else. Was Mum trying to run away from a failed relationship? Removing herself so that he couldn't come around and pick her up again whenever he felt like it? But *Liverpool*?

Then there was the burglary. It had happened a couple of months before and it had upset her badly. Every night for weeks she'd gone round double-checking the locks. She'd got hold of a cricket bat from somewhere and had it by her bed. It had unnerved her. Living with a garden backing on to the forest was an invitation to thieves, she'd said. Eventually she'd insisted on having a new bolt and padlock put on the back gate. Since then she'd *seemed* happier.

Was it those two things together that had made her think about moving?

It slowly dawned on me that there was an unusual amount of noise outside. It seemed to be coming in through the back door but I could tell it was from the street out front. Car doors slammed and there were voices calling. After a few moments of listening to it I went out to see what was happening.

Parked across the road was the van that was laying cable down the length of the street. It was bright orange, with the words *CommLink* in vivid green. I tutted. It had been giving me a headache for days. That and the fact that the pavements were dug up, making it difficult to get to and fro.

Our neighbour Gloria was outside talking to Mrs Simpson, the lady from across the road. Gloria looked as she usually did. Today she was wearing a yellow cheesecloth dress that showed her tanned shoulders, her skin like leather. Even though it was early in the morning she had all her make-up on and her hair curled. She was over sixty but tried to look twenty years younger. It didn't work. Mrs Simpson, with her regular old-lady clothes, looked fresher.

"Something's up with one of the Henderson kids," Gloria said.

"Arrested, you think?" Mrs Simpson said. "It's not the first time!"

"Out of control, that family. Out till all hours. I saw the nine-year-old up the forest last week, on her own, at gone ten o'clock."

They continued talking and I glanced up the street at the two police cars parked neatly one after the other. I wondered if one of the kids had been arrested and why. Drugs? Robbery? Whatever it was, it didn't usually take two police cars to announce it. Maybe it was something more dramatic. The Hendersons always seemed to be on the edge of something dodgy.

They lived eight doors down from us. Number 40, Forest Lane. We didn't really know the family well but you couldn't miss them whenever you walked up and down the street. Mr Henderson was often fixing cars outside his house. There was usually a vehicle jacked up by the pavement and he was half under it. Mrs Simpson said it was illegal and that he was running a business from a residential address, but nothing was ever done. His wife, a giant woman who wore tent-like dresses, always seemed to be pregnant. They had five children and one on the way. The youngest, Jade, was a toddler, who was often sitting in the front seat of the car her dad was working on. The older children were not nice. One of them, a surly boy called Vince, was in year ten at my school. The rest were at primary, although one of them went to special school. No one was quite sure why.

My mum didn't like the family much. Nobody seemed to have a good word to say about them. The fact that two police cars were parked outside their house was not a surprise to anyone.

"That boy, Vincent?" Gloria said, running her fingers through the top of her hair. "He's not right in the head!"

Mrs Simpson's attention was further up the street. She moved her head so that she could have a better look.

"Another police car!" she said.

I looked. This time it was an ordinary black car. Two men and a woman got out of it.

"How do you know?" I said.

"You can tell the police by the way they walk," Mrs Simpson said. "Tall and upright. Like they're in charge."

A door opened further up the street.

"Hi, Raymond!" Gloria shouted.

Raymond was wearing shorts and a T-shirt that didn't meet in the middle. He stood for a moment and looked at the police cars up the road.

"Those Hendersons!" Gloria said in a loud voice.

He gave a wave before he got into a small black van that had an old Victorian bathtub painted on the side. He revved up and then sped off up the street. Some people from across the way were looking out of their windows.

"Oh well," I said, giving a last look up the street.

"I'll let you know if I hear anything," Gloria said.

I went indoors. I could hear the sound of the radio from the bathroom upstairs. Mum was up. I filled the kettle and got some bread out for toast. Then I heard a distant beeping sound. My mobile. I stood very still and listened. It came again, from the direction of the living room. I went in and looked around. It was lying on the carpet by the sofa. I tutted. I was always leaving it in places and forgetting to put it on charge. I saw the message icon. I scrolled down and saw the names *Susie* and *Grace*, my school friends, and then *Robbie*. I opened his text.

Call me when you get a chance. Rob.

I put the mobile in my pocket. I was in no mood for a conversation with my boyfriend. I plodded up the stairs as my mum emerged from the bathroom in a cloud of steam. She gave me an uncertain smile and went into her room. I followed her in and sat on her bed as she got dressed. There was an uncomfortable silence. I sat there anyway. I felt she owed me some sort of explanation. She looked at me a couple of times as if she was going to say something. When she had her trousers and blouse on she finally spoke.

"I should have phoned last night. I'm sorry."

She leant forward to her mirror and dabbed make-up on to her cheeks.

"Where were you?"

She got her lipstick out. She paused as if she was considering her words.

"I went to Gerry's. There were some things I wanted to say to him. Don't look at me like that. Gerry's an idiot, I know that. I am fond of him, though."

She turned back to the mirror and put her lipstick on. Then she snapped the case shut and walked across to her handbag and began putting things into it.

"You were so drunk!" I said, folding my arms. "Don't you think it's dangerous? Walking round in the middle of the night? In that state!"

She sat on the bed and pulled on some shoes. Then she looked at me and put her hand on my leg. I could smell her perfume.

"Stel, I know I've been drinking too much lately. I know I shouldn't get involved with losers like Gerry. I know I should eat more fruit and vegetables and clean the cooker more often. But I never said I was mother of the year. I am what I am."

"I'm just worried about you," I said, feeling awkward, as if it were me who had been acting badly, not her.

"I'm a big girl. I can look after myself."

"Shall I make you some breakfast?" I said.

"Haven't got time, love," she said.

"You should eat *something*. I could bring you up some orange juice," I said.

She turned to me and gave me a look of exasperation.

"I'll get something on my way to work. I'll be fine. You don't have to worry and fuss about me."

"Are you seeing Gerry again?"

"I don't know. Maybe. Probably not. I just don't know.

What I need is a nice young man like Robbie," she said, standing up, ruffling her fingers through my hair. "Dependable, decent, clever. You should hold on to him."

Her words irked me and I found myself looking down at the floor where her wet clothes from the previous night were lying in a pile. I reached out and scooped them up. Her skirt was covered in mud. So were her shoes and T-shirt. Even her bag looked like it had been trailing along the ground.

"Did you fall over last night?" I said, standing up, holding the clothes out as evidence.

"Enough, Stel," she said, her face changing, her expression hardening. She took my arm and steered me towards the door. She was smaller than I was by four or five centimetres but her grip was strong. "You make me feel totally inadequate. At work I'm a manager. There I am *important*. Here I am constantly in the wrong!"

The door shut. I stood in the hallway for a moment feeling silly. The front doorbell sounded. I draped her things over the banister and went downstairs, my shoulders stiff with tension. Through the glass I could see the shape of Gloria's yellow dress.

"One of the Hendersons has gone missing, that's why there's so many police up there. One of the children. In the night, apparently. I must get on, see you later."

Mum came down the stairs holding her briefcase. Avoiding eye contact I mumbled about what had happened to the Hendersons. She was quiet for a moment; then she put her hand on my shoulder and spoke.

"Let's not fall out, Stel," she said, "you're my best mate!"

"I found the letter about the Liverpool job," I said. "Why didn't you even tell me about that?"

"I only got that yesterday!" she said. "We can talk about it tonight."

She gave me a lipstick kiss on my cheek and went out the front door.

Later I went into my bedroom.

The breeze was making the net curtain billow. I stepped across to the window and looked out. The forest looked bigger somehow, the dense foliage reaching out, as if it had spread further overnight, the edges of it licking over the garden fences. I stuck my head out and looked along the houses to see if I could see the Hendersons' garden along the way, but it was just too far. I realized then that I hadn't asked Gloria which of the Hendersons had gone missing. Vince from year ten? Or the funny brother who went to special school? No doubt whoever it was would turn up later having wasted everyone's time.

I tossed my mobile on the bed. I never gave the Hendersons another thought. They weren't my problem.

THREE

The toddler, Jade, had been taken. Snatched from her cot. It happened sometime in the night, between eleven and two. The Hendersons' house was one of a group of bungalows in the lower end of the road. The little girl went to bed just before nine, they said. She'd fallen asleep in front of the telly so Mr Henderson had carried her out to the bedroom at the back of the house, which she shared with her sister, a girl of eight. He managed to lay her in her cot without waking her up. The eight-year-old wasn't there; she was staying at a friend's house. Mrs Henderson checked on the girl about eleven. By midnight most of the family were in bed. Only Vincent was up watching a DVD.

The windows were open in every room. That wasn't unusual. Everyone's windows were open because of the heat. When the rain started about two, it woke Mr Henderson up and he went round the house shutting them. When he went into Jade's room he almost didn't look, just crept across the floor and pulled the window over. Then he saw that the side of Jade's cot was down and Jade wasn't there. At first he thought the toddler had woken up and got herself out. He went round to the other bedrooms and looked. Then he looked at the cot again.

Vincent was lying asleep on the sofa, the DVD player still running.

Mr Henderson looked in cupboards and under beds. He tried to stay calm. He was careful. He went outside, into the garden, looked in the shed, behind the bushes. He opened the gate that led to the forest path at the back of the house in case the toddler had been sleepwalking or was playing a game of some sort.

Then he panicked and woke up his wife.

I heard this story about ten. I was doing the washing and ironing. It was one of my weekly jobs. Wash the clothes, dry them, iron them. I'd been all around the house collecting dirty stuff, divided it up and started the wash loads. The rain of the previous night had left the air fresher and I intended to hang it all on the line outside.

Two different people called and told me the story. Mrs Simpson came to the door and seemed to whisper it, looking up and down the street as though she were telling me state secrets. She said that the little girl had been wearing her giraffe pyjamas and that her favourite monkey toy had been taken as well. I had no idea how she knew these things. Gloria knocked later and walked straight in, sitting herself on a kitchen chair, and going over all the details she'd heard. Mrs Henderson, she said, had slept right through it, like a beached whale. Gloria's face was twisted up in condemnation, as though Mrs Henderson's deep sleep was to blame.

I turned the washing machine on and went out into the street. The first person I saw was Raymond, unloading some tools from the back of his van.

"All right, kid?" he said, walking towards me, a couple of dustsheets hanging over his arm.

"Um. . ."

I hated it that he called me *kid*. He'd done it for years and I really wished I could say something to him about it, like, *I'm all grown up now? And I have a name?* But he was a family friend and it was something I had to put up with.

"They found tracks of an SUV in the forest near the Hendersons' back garden. People are saying that the baby was taken."

"Why?" I said, puzzled.

Raymond gave a little shrug. He knew why and I knew why but neither of us wanted to say it.

"See you later," he said, walking back towards his van.

I walked out into the middle of the road and looked down towards the Hendersons'. There seemed to be a lot of activity. I could see crime scene tapes across the front of the house and a variety of cars parked with people sitting in them, or standing outside, leaning on the roofs, looking up towards the Hendersons' house. I guessed it was the press.

I went back indoors and put the twenty-four-hour news station on. I had to wait a while, watching world news and sport and weather, but eventually the story came on. It was the first item on the midday bulletin.

A fifteen-month-old girl has been snatched from her cot while her parents slept in the next room. It happened at a house on the edge of Epping Forest in Essex.

The newsreader was a woman. Her expression was

deadly serious, unlike moments before, when she was joking with someone about the weather and the hosepipe ban. She carried on as a photograph of the toddler appeared on the screen. I looked at it and for the first time felt this horrible feeling in my stomach. It was a recent picture of Jade Henderson. Her cheeks were round as bubbles and her eyes were dark. She had a mildly surprised expression on her face, her mouth open in a small "O". I remembered then that I had picked her up recently when I was walking past her house. She'd been with her brother Vince in the front garden and just as I passed, Jade had staggered off the end of the path and rolled on to the pavement. Vince had been sitting sulkily reading a magazine and rose up as soon as it happened. But I was there so I scooped her up.

The little girl was chunky and hot and smelled of milk and banana. On the pavement was a tatty brown monkey. Vince picked it up, throwing a worried look back into the house. No doubt he didn't want his mum to know that the baby had gone outside the garden.

Without a word I handed her over and walked up to my house.

The news had gone on to something else but there was still a strip of red across the bottom of the screen with the words BREAKING NEWS *Essex Toddler abducted*.

I heard the bell and went to the front door thinking it was Gloria or Mrs Simpson. It was Robbie. He was standing back from the door, almost halfway down the path, as if he wasn't quite sure whether he'd be welcome.

"Hi!" I said uncertainly.

"I heard about the baby on the telly. Thought I'd come round."

I nodded and held the door open so that he would come in. He gave me a look as if to say, *Sure I can come in?*

"Come in!" I said, mildly irritated by his timidity.

Robbie Simms. My boyfriend. Why was it that I was only in his company for moments before he irritated me?

"Do you want a drink?" I said. "We could sit in the garden."

He nodded and leant back against the unit as I got the glasses out. He was wearing khaki shorts and a long T-shirt. He had his satchel over his shoulder, a canvas bag that I had bought him from Gap and now hated. He'd loved it immediately and took it everywhere. He said he needed it to carry a book and a bottle of water round with him. Whenever we were on a bus or a tube he'd fish out his book: *Crime and Punishment, 1984, Catch-22*. He'd read a page or two while we travelled, then turn the corner down and put it back in the bag. I'd tried, on several occasions, to persuade him to leave it at the bottom of his wardrobe but it always turned up again, hanging off his shoulder, looking like a bag that a girl might carry. Why had I bought it?

"Any news on the baby?"

I told him what I'd heard while I poured a couple of glasses of drink.

"You take these out and I'll follow," I said, noticing that the wash cycle had finished. I squatted down and pulled the wet clothes out of the tub and into the basket.

He sat on the garden bench while I pegged up the clothes. Big things up the far end where the sun would hit the garden later in the day. I stood on tiptoes for a moment to see if I could spy any activity from the Hendersons' garden but there were too many trees and bushes even to pinpoint where it was. I pegged up my mum's skirt and top that she had worn the previous evening. Then I got down to underwear, my mum's pale lacy bras and pants which contrasted with my no-nonsense whites. I didn't look round at Robbie. I answered his questions about the police while shaking out and pinning up pair after pair of my pants and my bras. I felt a growing embarrassment and tried to talk as loudly as I could to show I wasn't aware of what I was doing. All of a sudden there was quiet and a second later he was behind me, his arms around my waist.

"I thought you'd call me," he said.

I tensed at his touch.

"I didn't find your message till a while ago. You know what I'm like with my mobile," I said, turning round to face him, stepping back, out of his arms, the washing basket in between us.

"Come for a walk up to High Beach."

"I've got a lot to do today."

It wasn't true. I could have gone. But High Beach was a romantic place for us and lately I hadn't felt like going there.

"Come this evening. It'll be cooler then."

"Actually, Mum and me are having a talk tonight," I said. "She's applying for a new job."

I thought of something then. If Mum did get a job in Liverpool it would mean I would move away from Robbie. I wouldn't see him again.

"You could come round my house after?"

"I might," I said, sidestepping him and walking back towards the French doors, "when we've finished."

The doorbell sounded and I quickened my step.

"Who's that?" I said, glad of the interruption. Guilt settled on me as soon as I put the washing basket down and began to walk up the hallway. Poor Robbie. He couldn't see that my feelings had changed.

A dark blue shape moved through the glass. The police.

"Good morning, miss. WPC Gwen Fisher. You're probably aware of the sad events that we're dealing with this morning. I'm just checking who is resident at this address at present and whether you have any information for us at this time. I'm doing all the houses and may well revisit later as events develop."

She said it like a speech and then paused. I noticed that she had a sticking plaster on her earlobe.

"Me and my mum live here. Teresa Parfitt – that's my mum – and me, Stella Parfitt. Mum's at work, though."

"And this young man?"

Robbie had walked up the hall behind me.

"This is. . . This is Robbie Simms . . . my boyfriend."

"OK. Did you see anything odd? In the street? In the gardens? Last evening?"

I shook my head.

"And what time will your mother be home from work?"

"About six?"

"An officer will call back to speak to her. Thank you for your time. Good afternoon."

The WPC turned and walked down the path, then went to the next house. I stood at the door and Robbie patted his bag.

"I'll be off then," he said. "Might see you tonight?"

He leant down to give me a kiss on the lips. I stretched up. Our mouths met for half a second, then I backed off. He walked past, the silly shoulder bag swinging round as he went out of the gate, passing the WPC as she went into yet another house.

I went back indoors, glad to be on my own. In the garden I finished hanging out the washing and thought hard about the previous evening. Had I noticed anything odd? Nothing occurred to me apart from the fact that Mum was out late. Maybe I should have told the WPC that Mum wasn't even in. Now the police would come back to speak to her and she wouldn't be able to tell them a thing because she hadn't even been at home.

But maybe, by then, I thought, the police will have found Jade Henderson.

FOUR

The police arrived about seven. Mum had only just got in from work so I'd not had time to tell her they were coming. She'd rung during the day and I'd told her all about the missing toddler. She'd hardly said a word, sounded distracted. She asked me if Gerry had phoned and I told her he hadn't.

She was in the shower when they knocked.

I had expected the same WPC or just another uniformed officer. Instead there was a man and a woman. The man was youngish in a light-coloured suit. The woman was older with stiff blonde hair. They showed their identification and introduced themselves and then asked if they could speak to Teresa Parfitt. I held the door open for them.

"She's just in the shower," I said. "Why don't you wait in the kitchen?"

They were friendly, thanking me. They walked on and I ran up the stairs. The bathroom door was hanging open so I went to my mum's bedroom. She'd changed into her jeans and a T-shirt. She was sitting on the bed sorting through one of her jewellery boxes. On the bed were several necklaces and pairs of earrings.

"Have you borrowed my blue bangle, Stel? The one with the painted flowers on?"

I shook my head.

"The police are here," I said, "I should have told you. They're asking all the neighbours about last night? I know you were out but. . ."

My mum's forehead crinkled.

"I don't suppose they'll take long," I said.

She looked up at me and her face had an odd expression. I couldn't make it out. It was as if she was annoyed. She swore quietly. She grabbed up the beads and put them in the box. The earrings followed. I shrugged. I felt as if I'd done something wrong.

"I'll be down in a minute," she said tersely, running her fingers through her hair. "Make them a cup of tea."

I left her and went downstairs. The woman was seated at the kitchen table, the man was standing up, looking at the screen of his mobile. They both turned down the tea. They'd probably had gallons of it if they'd been doing house-to-house enquiries all day long.

"Really terrible about Jade Henderson," I said, feeling that I should say something.

The woman nodded.

"I don't suppose there's any news?"

She shook her head. I heard Mum on the stairs. When the kitchen door opened Mum stood there wearing completely different clothes; a dark skirt and white shirt, as if she were going for a job interview. She had black sandals on but no tights.

26

"I'm Teresa Parfitt," she said. "I understand you'd like to talk to me."

The woman police officer stood up. She gave a crinkly smile.

"Are you the Teresa Parfitt who used to reside at Little Madden in North Yorkshire?"

I frowned. Little Madden? What did my mum's childhood home have to do with anything?

My mum looked composed, much calmer than she had been upstairs. I noticed then that she had combed her hair flat and wasn't wearing any jewellery.

"I wondered how long it would take you to come and find me," she said.

"What's going on?" I said, feeling a bit stupid.

"Can I have a minute to talk to my daughter?"

The woman nodded.

"Come into the hall," my mum said, taking me by the elbow.

I pulled back, not liking this one bit. Mum edged me on, the man moving so that I could get past. I had this odd feeling. Like I was a small child being taken away from the adults. It annoyed me. Once out in the hallway I stood completely still.

"What's going on?" I demanded.

"I've got to talk to these police officers. It won't take long. It's all to do with something that happened years ago and when they go I'll tell you all about it."

"What?" I said. "Tell me now!"

"I can't. It'd take too long. Don't worry about me. I'm

not upset. I've not done anything wrong. I'll just talk to them and when they go I'll tell you everything. Trust me."

She pushed me on, away from the kitchen.

"You go upstairs. When you hear them leave, come down."

"Mum!" I said.

"We'll talk about it. And the Liverpool job."

"But. . ."

The kitchen door closed and I heard the mumble of voices. There was nothing else for me to do except go upstairs. I went into my room and gave the door a half-hearted bang.

Little Madden?

What did Mum's birthplace have to do with Jade Henderson?

I stood by the window and looked out along the gardens. I could only see about four along. There were some big trees and bushes that obscured the view of the rest. I caught the smell of a barbecue. I rolled my eyes to no one in particular. Life carried on no matter what happened. I stared into the forest beyond. The gardens were tiny in comparison, their fences overwhelmed by the weight of the trees, as if the forest was intent on forcing its way in.

There had been a wood at Little Madden, the village my mum grew up in. She'd described it to me. It was nowhere near as big as Epping but you could still get lost in it, she'd said. I'd never been there. My nana and grandad had moved away so there was no reason for us to visit the wood or the town.

She told me bits and pieces about her childhood in Little Madden. It always started with a question from me. *Where did you go to school, Mum? What was your street like? Who was your best friend?* Her answers were quick; she didn't sit back and launch into a long story.

Nana and Grandad were more enthusiastic. They told me about the house they had had there, the church they used to go to, about the village up the road that was called Great Madden and how there used to be a big house in between the two places called Madden Hall.

But I had never been there. Mum hadn't wanted to go, even though we lived at Whitby, which was only twenty miles away. On our way to Nana and Grandad's we often passed a marker that said *Little Madden 2m*. Mum always drove by.

When Mum's own grandad died and left us his house, Mum sold it and we moved south and ended up in Epping. It meant that we didn't see Nana and Grandad much. When I asked Mum why, she explained it in various ways. They lived far away. They didn't like to travel. They were church people and very busy. It was a long way for us to go and anyway Mum had a busy job and couldn't afford the time. We tried to see them around Christmas.

Mum had a way of keeping information close to her chest. Talking about her family and her childhood was not her favourite thing. I always had to ask. She never volunteered. Eventually I asked her about my father. Her account was typically brief.

He was a bloke I met in a pub. He gave me a lift home. I was twenty. I made a big mistake. I ended up being pregnant. I didn't even know his second name.

End of story.

Mum's history was slight. As if she were filling in an arduous form and was only telling the bits that were absolutely necessary.

I heard some movement from below, chairs scraping along the floor. I went out on to the landing and listened. It sounded friendly enough. The door opened and I stepped back into my room as the police officer walked along the hallway. I heard them say something about seeing my mum at ten o'clock the next morning. Then the front door closed. I walked out to the top of the stairs. Mum turned and saw me.

"Come down," she said, "there's something you need to know."

FIVE

I didn't want to sit down while she told her story. It was partly annoyance. I wanted to be physically higher than she was so that she had to talk up to me. How typical was it that there was something important in her life that I didn't know about? I was seventeen. Old enough for her to cry to me when Gerry Boyd let her down and yet I was still in the dark about her past.

Like the Liverpool job. I learned about everything afterwards.

She fiddled with the buttons on her blouse.

"Sit down, Stel," she said.

I shook my head.

"Suit yourself. Cup of tea?"

I shook my head again.

"Well, I want one."

"You stay there, I'll make it. You can start the story."

I didn't want her faffing about with cups and teabags. I wanted her to get on with it. I picked up the kettle, filled it at the tap and clicked it on. Then I turned back and stood with my arms folded across my chest. My mum started to talk, her words coming out quickly, as though she wanted to get it over and done with.

"When I was eighteen I took a neighbour's baby into Little Madden woods for a walk and someone stole her from me. That's it."

I waited, her words barely sinking in.

"That's it," she said. "I was doing a favour for a neighbour. Looking after her little girl. Someone took her from me. You know, snatched her. For a while the police didn't believe me but then they did. It was a terrible thing. An awful time. Not really something that I wanted to tell anyone about."

The kettle boiled. The click sounded sharp as it turned itself off. I waited. My mum was making it sound like a tiny incident. Like taking a baby for a walk in the woods and losing its sock. I pulled a chair out and sat down.

"I want to know it all, from the beginning. Every detail."

"I'll need that cup of tea," she said, looking over at the kettle and the ribbons of steam coming from it.

Five minutes later, holding a mug with both hands, she told me the story.

"We lived next door to this hopeless woman. Jackie Gilbert. She had three kids; two boys of about six or seven and a baby girl. She was a classic case. No husband, no job; just one kid after another. I think she was only about twenty-two when she moved in. You know how Nana and Grandad were big church people? Roman Catholics, always doing good deeds. If they weren't praying they were cleaning or fund-raising or giving their opinion on important issues. When Jackie Gilbert moved next door they had someone to look after. My mum helped her with housework and organizing the kids. My dad did odd bits of decorating and took the two older boys to play football. I sometimes babysat or took the baby for a walk to give Jackie time on her own. For months they were always in our house or my parents were in hers. Then she met this bloke, Kirk. He was only a teenager, about nineteen, I think. Out of work, of course. Within weeks he'd moved in with her, so my mum and dad stayed away. They still helped out with the kids but it was clear that Jackie had moved on from them. I still took the baby out from time to time. I think Jackie was glad of the break. Eventually it became obvious that she was pregnant again."

The kitchen was quiet. Outside it was beginning to get dark.

"Jackie seemed to go off her other kids. The two older boys still spent time with my dad but the younger one, the toddler, was neglected. She was eighteen months, walking, quite a sturdy little girl but I saw her often on her own wandering round the back garden, like a dog that had been let out of the house for some exercise. Sometimes the older kids were there, sometimes they weren't. She looked dirty as well, still in nappies, of course. So Jackie let me look after her a lot. I used to take her up to the woods in her pushchair, often in the afternoon. It was summer, like this, hot. I liked looking after her. Lizzie, she was called. A sweet little girl. When I took her home again Jackie would call for one of the boys to take her or leave her in her bedroom alone. Kirk had no interest in the little girl. He was only interested in *his* baby."

"This Lizzie, she was the baby who was. . ."

My mum nodded.

"It was a Tuesday afternoon. My exams were over so I offered to take her out. We walked up into the woods. We went along the usual paths. I didn't see any kids because it was a school day. It was hot, stiflingly hot. We walked off the main path to get into the shaded parts of the wood. I remember feeling the chill of the shadows and it was lovely and Lizzie must have fallen asleep. I think I sat down for a while. Maybe I even dozed. The police said I must have. They said that I'd been up in the woods for nearly four hours but it didn't feel like that. . ."

She stopped. I looked expectant.

"That's it, really. I walked back on to the path and a car pulled up suddenly. It came from nowhere. One minute the wood was silent and empty and then it was there. I just stood still waiting for it to go on, to pass, but a man got out and pushed me away from the pushchair. He took the baby out. She was still sleeping, I'm sure. He took her out and put her into the car. I must have been on the ground because none of this bit is very clear to me. I do know that when I got up the car was gone and Lizzie was gone and all that was left was the pushchair."

She stopped, her lips pursed.

"I must have wandered for a while. I think I started to hear the sound of other kids, you know, playing after school was over. After a while, I suppose it was a long while, I walked to the police house with the empty pushchair and told them."

"They didn't believe you?" I said.

"That didn't become obvious for a few days. I took them up to the woods, showed them where it happened, or where I thought it happened. They questioned me for hours and hours. They took my clothes, they took my purse, my book, all the things I'd had with me. They allowed me to go and stay with Grandad in Whitby. They said it was better if I kept away from the village. Eventually, after about a week, I think, they told me they thought I'd made it all up. They said they didn't think I'd. . ."

My mum paused.

"They didn't think I'd *killed* the baby. They weren't saying that. They thought that something had happened to the baby. Maybe it choked on something and I panicked and buried it in the woods somewhere."

My mum's lips had thinned, her mouth bunched up.

"Oh, Mum," I said.

I pushed my chair back and moved next to her. I held her arm.

"As if I could have hurt the baby!" she said, looking at me.

Her eyes glassed over and she immediately put her hand across them.

"I am not going to cry over this again. It was twenty years ago. I did nothing to that baby. I was accused wrongly and I spent months of my life suffering for it. I'm not going to start it all again now!"

I shuffled to the side and put my arm around her shoulder. She seemed to shrink down into the chair.

"Maybe I should have told you before but honestly, when do you start a conversation like that with your daughter? When she's five? Ten? Twelve? It just never came up and there seemed no *reason* to tell you."

I gave her a hug. Her skin felt hot, her shoulder felt bony. Her mug of tea sat hardly touched.

"Did they ever find her?"

She shook her head decisively.

"Poor Mum," I said.

I wasn't angry any more. I gave her a kiss on the cheek and then stood up, moving her mug to the sink. I thought of the baby in the wood. I pictured it in a pushchair and then, as I rinsed the mug, the pushchair was empty. It gave me an odd feeling. I pictured the wood full of police officers, staring down at the ground looking for clues. Then something awful occurred to me. I turned to her.

"They're not saying you had anything to do with Jade Henderson?"

She stood up and shook her head. She picked up the wet mug and pulled the tea towel from the side and began to dry it.

"I don't think so. They've probably taken hundreds of names: friends, neighbours, tradesmen, anyone around really. My name is on some computer database somewhere and here I am living in the same street as the missing baby. You can't blame them for coming to see me."

"Did you tell them you were at Gerry Boyd's?"

She nodded. She was still drying the mug. I took it off her and put it in the cupboard.

"I told the police I left his place about twelve and walked home. Now they just want me to go down to the station and give a statement."

She put her arms around me and pushed her face into my shoulder.

"I would never have hurt Lizzie," she said.

"I know."

Using my free hand I fluffed her hair up.

"What about the Liverpool job?"

"I applied for that job the day after me and Gerry finished. Weeks ago. I didn't think I stood a chance. I'll ring them tomorrow and tell them I'm not interested."

"That's a relief!"

"Well," she said, turning to the cupboard, picking out a stemmed glass. "This calls for a large glass of something."

I picked a bottle of red wine from the rack and set it on the table.

SIX

The next morning I made a sudden decision. I showered, dressed smartly and printed off a list of job agencies from the Internet. I had a quick breakfast, told Mum where I was going and headed for the tube station. Now that we weren't going to Liverpool I decided to follow up my original idea and get a job in an office, in the City or West End of London. Amid the upset of the events in the street and Mum's news it seemed a good idea to *do* something.

There was a train sitting in the station waiting to go. It filled up with commuters and then started up. Everyone had a seat. I knew that would change as we stopped at the twelve stations that led into town.

I stared out of the window watching the forest thin out, turn into open land and then into back gardens. I couldn't help but think of my mum all those years ago, taking the baby into the woods. She'd had long curly hair then. She'd looked quite different to me as a teenager, smaller and thinner, her face tiny, diminished by this great mop of hair that seemed to weigh down her head. She'd wheeled the baby into the woods and it had been stolen from her. I pictured a black car parked under a tree. Inside there was a man waiting for the pushchair to pass. Why?

The train chugged on. We were still above ground, passing a giant supermarket and an industrial estate. Standing in front of me was a young man with earphones, his head moving slightly, his eyes closed. I could hear his music, muffled, distant. Out of the window I could see a motorway and open fields. Soon the train would slide down into the underground tunnels. Then it would be black all the way to Bank.

Mum said there was a man in a black car. The police thought different. Mum had lied, they said, and buried the baby somewhere in the woods.

I thought of the forest that edged on to our house. It had been a kind of wonderland for me when I was younger; playing make-believe games, walking, running, hiding; making a den, hanging a rope to swing from a tree. As I got older it was a hideaway, a refuge, a place to go with my friends, Susie and Grace, a place to dawdle on my way home from school; somewhere to go with boyfriends, to kiss, to hug, to grapple. There were an infinite number of places to hide among the tree trunks, the bushes, the copses, the dips, the mounds. It was easy for a pair of teenagers to conceal themselves.

How much easier it would be to hide a baby.

I looked round and realized that we had gone underground. The carriage lights were yellow, the windows black. The train was thundering along, the sides of the tunnel flashing past.

The previous evening, after Mum had had a couple of glasses of wine, she told me about how the people in her village turned against her and her family. She'd only gone back to Madden once after the tragedy, but people had stared silently at her, neighbours and friends that she'd known all her life. Everybody had believed the worst.

And now the police were talking to her about Jade Henderson, asking her for an alibi. It made me feel angry.

Everyone called her Terri. She was petite and looked much younger than her 38 years. The long hair was gone and in its place was a short spiky cut. She worked in the offices of a national charity. She had an important job and was always bringing stuff home to do over the weekend, unpaid overtime. Out of work she was completely different. She dressed younger, showing her tattoo, piling on the make-up and jewellery. She had lots of friends and was always out somewhere. People liked her. Her only problem was with men. She attracted the wrong sort, like Gerry Boyd. When these relationships started to go wrong she became quiet and moody and kept herself to herself. When Gerry finished with her she started to drink red wine every night. She had a special crystal glass and during the evening she kept going out to the kitchen to fill it up. She rarely drank a whole bottle but there was never enough left to save. She went to pieces over men but she would never hurt anyone, let alone a child.

We stopped and the doors opened. More commuters came on to the train, making the existing passengers shuffle up closer to each other. I couldn't see through the people in front of me. I could only feel the train moving, shooting through the tunnels. The man beside me turned a page of his newspaper and I saw the headline BABE IN THE WOOD *Mystery of Essex Toddler*. I tried to read the first few lines but the man moved his position and I couldn't see. I looked at my watch and wondered how much longer it would take to get to where I was going.

The tube pulled into Bank station about ten minutes later. After some faffing about in my bag I found my Oyster card. When I got above ground the sun was out, making me blink. The city was hot; the buildings looked caked and cracked. The traffic sat mumbling on the roads. I could taste the exhaust fumes. I looked at my printout, my *A to Z* of London and went on my way to the first job agency.

It took most of the morning. Three agencies asked me to take some tests and undergo a kind of interview. They all looked very pleased with me and told me they'd let me know as soon as something suitable became available. I walked back through the city and thought about myself working there, every day.

It wasn't what Mum wanted. She wanted me to stay on at school until year thirteen and finish my A levels. She wanted me to go to university and get a degree. I'd heard it from other people as well; my teachers, Susie, Grace and Robbie. I didn't want it. In the last couple of years I'd felt like my school rucksack was full of lead, weighing me down, keeping me stuck in the past; a name on a register, Stella Parfitt, year twelve, schoolgirl.

In the end Mum said it was up to me, it was my decision.

Before going down into the Bank underground station I decided to give her a call and tell her what had happened and also to find out how things had gone at the police station. I searched in my bag for my mobile but it wasn't there. I thought back to the morning and tutted. I'd left it downstairs by the sink when I'd been getting breakfast. I was always leaving it places.

I bought some food and an afternoon paper. Once on the tube going home I took it out to read. The inside page was full of the missing toddler. The headline was BABY VANISHED. And there were pictures of Epping Forest. It looked wild and dense, like a wilderness. *Is Baby Jade Lost in the Woods?* the sub-heading said. *Could she have wandered out of the house on her own?*

I read the article. There were no details that I hadn't already heard. Raymond, my neighbour, had said something about a man in an SUV, but the report didn't mention that. It went over the course of events. It had diagrams of the bungalow, showing all the bedrooms and where the members of the family slept. It showed the garden and the forest beyond. The bungalow was in black and white but the forest was several shades of green. It gave depth and life and contrasted with the line drawing of the house. There were photographs of Mr and Mrs Henderson holding a monkey toy *just like the one that went missing with Jade* and a photograph of the giraffe pyjamas, a new pair spread out on a table to show the design.

There was no real new information, no clues or statements from the police to suggest that they had any idea what had happened to the little girl. The police said that they were *following several lines of enquiry*. One of those lines had been calling at my house and talking to my mum about something that had happened twenty years ago.

I had to change at Leytonstone and wait for the Epping line. When I got back on, the train was mostly empty. I took out the sandwiches I'd bought. I picked the top one out and slotted the pointed end into my mouth. The train was still above ground, moving sluggishly as though it wasn't in a hurry. When I finished eating I looked around. Further down the carriage was a couple. The girl was wearing skimpy clothes, shorts and a halter top. The thing that caught my eye was that she was also wearing *boots*. It made me feel hotter to look at her and I fanned myself with the newspaper. I noticed the boy then and realized that I knew him. It was Jack Slater, a boy from my school, who'd left the previous year. He was reading a magazine. He was wearing light-coloured trousers and an open-neck shirt. His hair was longer than I remembered and he looked tanned. The girl with the boots had her arm through his and was talking into his ear. From time to time he smiled at something she said but he never lifted his eyes off the page. When the train pulled into Debden station they got up. He didn't look in my direction. I considered calling his name and saying hello but he had his back to me and the girl had her thumb hooked over the waistband of his trousers. It gave me an odd feeling, a curl of excitement in my stomach. I stared down at my newspaper without saying anything and they got off. When I looked up I caught his eye through the window. He frowned and then gave a wave; the girl looked puzzled. I waved back as the train speeded up.

When the train finally arrived at Epping I got out and started the walk back home. I was thinking about the interviews and about seeing Jack Slater and I was in good spirits. As I approached Forest Lane I began to feel a little bit apprehensive. My footsteps slowed a little and I tensed. The missing child's family were nearby. How could I be light-hearted when there was such sadness a few doors away from where I lived? I didn't really know them and what I did know I didn't like much. Still, I felt awful for what had happened, and when I turned into my road my shoulders were rigid and my previous good mood gone. I expected to see the same numbers of police and journalists that I had seen the previous day.

They were all there; if anything there were more of them. The worrying thing was that some of them had moved. They were no longer outside the Hendersons' house.

They were further up the road. Outside my house.

SEVEN

I speeded up. The crowd were mostly the same people who had been hanging round for the past couple of days. Neighbours, too. I saw Mrs Simpson at her gate. Gloria was there, standing out in an alarming pink tracksuit. I half raised my hand to wave but something about their faces, their expressions, stopped me. As I approached the crowd seemed to quieten and then, one by one, two by two, they turned in my direction. I glanced at my house and saw that all the blinds were down.

"Are you the daughter of Teresa Parfitt?" a woman said, thrusting her face in front of me.

"Can you comment on the fact that your mother was interviewed by police in connection with the disappearance of Jade Henderson?" another demanded.

"Has your mother been acting oddly recently?"

"Have you ever been to Little Madden Wood?"

The questions flashed in front of me, loud and dazzling, as if lit up.

I didn't answer; I just looked around at the faces. Just then my front door opened and the people closest to the fence turned away from me and started to shout towards the house.

"Teresa Parfitt!"

"Teresa, come out and talk to us!"

"Teresa Parfitt! Do you know anything about Jade?"

But it was just Robbie Simms standing there. He beckoned to me and I put my head down and walked in his direction, sidestepping the people who tried to stop me by pushing into my path. I noticed Raymond, standing by the back of his van, looking perplexed.

"Excuse me!" I said several times, finally reaching the gate and going inside, as the journalists' questions flew around me like midges.

"Come on!" Robbie said.

I was at the door. I walked in. He shut it rapidly behind me.

"What was that?" I said, pointing backwards.

"It's been like this since lunch time. Your mum tried to call you but. . ."

I looked up the stairs. Mum was sitting on the top stair, her elbows on her knees. Her face looked puffy, as if she'd been crying.

"I left my mobile here."

"The press know about what happened, where your mum used to live and stuff. She was looking for you so she rang me. I came round. She told me all about it," Robbie said.

They knew about the stolen baby. That's why they were outside. I looked up the stairs. Mum had moved away. I heard her footsteps and the back bedroom door close.

"Did you ring the police?" I said.

It wasn't legal, was it? That journalists could just march up to your house like some invading army?

"We did. The police said to stay low. That the journalists would give up if nobody reacted to them. They say they can't arrest them, they're not breaking any law."

Robbie shrugged as if it were beyond comprehension. He was wearing a faded T-shirt that I hadn't seen before. It was scruffy. I looked down at myself in my smart city clothes. He was such a mess. On the ground I saw his Gap bag and it infuriated me.

"You should have done something. Got rid of them!"

"How?" he said, shrugging his shoulders. "What could I have done?"

Why was I being such an ungrateful bitch? In the back of my head I could hear the noise of the conversations that were going on outside the front door. I couldn't make out any words, just a drone with occasional dips and highs.

"I'm upset," I said. "I don't know what to say." I reached out and touched his arm. "Could you make us a cup of tea? And I'll go up and see Mum?"

He nodded and moved backwards away from me. I went upstairs. The spare room overlooked the back garden and was the furthest point from the street. Mum was lying on the single bed, her knees up to her chest.

"Mum!" I said, sitting down, rubbing her shoulder. "They'll go away. They'll get fed up. They'll realize that there's nothing in the story!"

"They won't. Now that they know they'll never leave us

alone. This is what happened twenty years ago. Why'd you think I never went back to Little Madden?"

She sat up and pulled a couple of tissues from a box on the floor.

"Every time I left Grandad's house there was some journalist hanging round trying to get the real story. They offered me money. Thousands of pounds. They asked me to take a pushchair up into the woods for photographs. They wouldn't leave me alone."

"But this is different," I said.

"How is it?"

"This has got nothing to do with you. In Little Madden you were part of it. You were a victim. Here you're not even involved."

"In Little Madden they didn't think I was a victim. They thought I was a criminal."

"This is different!" I said, through clenched teeth.

Our voices had dropped into whispers, as if we were afraid of being heard outside. I was half listening for Robbie's footsteps, hoping he'd come up with the tea. Then we could close the door and sit in the spare room until they all went home. But instead of hearing Robbie the noise from outside seemed to be getting louder.

"What's happening?" Mum said, gripping on to my arm. "Are there more people out there?"

Her face was crimson, one of her fists at her mouth, a bunched-up tissue sprouting out of it.

"No," I said, gently peeling her fingers away, "I'll go and look."

I ran into Mum's bedroom at the front of the house and looked out the side of the blind. There seemed to be more people there, and further along the street I could see a police car pulling up. Maybe they were taking it seriously at last. Maybe they would move everyone on.

But then I saw something that made my stomach drop. Mrs Henderson was coming along the street. She was wearing a big green dress that billowed out. She was walking slowly, puffing, as she usually did, and it looked as though Vincent was following her. Some of the journalists turned in her direction and started to run towards her. The noise level rose and as she came closer there were flashes from cameras and microphones were held out precariously in her direction. I let the blind drop and at that moment I heard Robbie come up the stairs.

"I need to get my mum away from here!" I said, in a low voice.

"You could come to my house. I'll get a taxi," Robbie said.

I nodded and took the tray of cups.

"You ring for one. Get them to come now. As soon as possible."

The doorbell rang. Once. Twice. Three times. Robbie was pressing buttons on his mobile. Mum appeared at the spare-room door.

"What's happened?" she said in a tiny voice.

"Have your tea," I said weakly.

The bell continued to ring, a single uninterrupted sound like someone drilling at the front door. Then it stopped and the silence was huge. You could hear the clock ticking from the living room downstairs.

Mrs Henderson's voice screamed through the front door. "What have you done with my baby! Where is she? Why did you take her? Give her back to me!"

We all froze and looked down the stairs. My mum cupped her hand over her mouth, turned and ran towards the bathroom. A moment later I heard her retching.

"Where's Jade?" Mrs Henderson wailed. "Where is my baby!"

Ten minutes later a police officer stood in the hallway as we waited for the taxi. He'd arrived quickly after the shouting began. He'd banged on the door and told us that Mrs Henderson had gone home. Robbie let him in while Mum and I stayed upstairs. He spoke about *Public Order Offences* and said it would *defuse the situation* if we went somewhere else for the night.

He'd said he'd wait with us for the taxi. My mum and I put a few things in a bag and we stood in the hallway while Robbie kept watch upstairs for the taxi. I'd expected the noise outside to lessen but it seemed to be louder; more voices, more car doors slamming. I was puzzled. Surely now that the police were involved the journalists would go home? They must have got some pictures of Mrs Henderson at our door.

"Taxi's here!"

Robbie's voice sounded from upstairs. Then he appeared, looking stony-faced.

"There's a bigger crowd out there," he said.

The policeman turned away and spoke into his radio.

"I've got a patrol coming," he said. "The sooner we move you the sooner this situation is under control."

He opened the front door and there was a surge of calling and shouting and booing. Mum grabbed on to my hand. The policeman stood in front. I was next, Mum was in the middle, Robbie was behind her. The policeman stood very still for a moment, like a headmaster wanting to quell a difficult class. The noise lessened but there were mumblings. I could see why the crowd had increased. It wasn't that more journalists had turned up. It was neighbours. Mrs Simpson and Gloria had been there from the start but there were other faces from further down the street. These were people we knew. Not *friends* but faces that we said hello to every day, people we would accept oversized mail for, acquaintances that we would wave to in the supermarket.

Why were they there?

Further up the street I could see the hazard lights of a saloon car blinking on and off. Our taxi. The policeman was shouting at everyone to *Move back!* And many of the people at the front, the journalists, did start to back away from the gate, but then a camper van pulled up across the road and a man and a woman and two teenagers got out of it. They looked vaguely familiar but I knew they weren't neighbours. They marched in our direction.

Later, when I remembered this, I pictured them rolling up their sleeves as though they were on their way to a fight but they weren't doing that. The teenagers in fact had their hands behind their backs and the woman had her arms crossed. She started swearing at us and then I recognized her. She was Mrs Henderson's sister; she lived a few streets away and her yellow camper van was often parked across someone's drive. She'd had stand-up rows in the street with other neighbours but this time she wasn't rowing with them. It was us she was shouting at.

"Go to the taxi," the policeman ordered and I moved away from him, pulling my mum along with me. I flinched at the verbal abuse that was shooting out of the woman's mouth, backed up by shouts of agreement from other people. The journalists in the middle looked gleeful, as though they'd dropped ten pence and found a fifty-pound note.

A brick hit our front window and the glass shattered. The noise shocked everyone for a moment and my mum let out a little yelp. I put my arm round her shoulder and edged her towards the taxi as the policeman shouted at the crowd. Robbie was behind her, his big body shielding her from the angry faces.

Then we heard the sound of an engine. The taxi was driving away. He didn't want to get mixed up in this. We were left standing in the street with nowhere to go.

"Here!" a voice shouted.

Raymond, our neighbour, had the doors of his van open. I pulled Mum towards it. We passed the Victorian bath design on the side and got in the back. We sat down beside boxes and pipes. Robbie got in the passenger seat.

No one said a word as we reversed up the street, the crowd in front getting smaller as we got further away. At the top of the road where the houses stopped and the forest began Raymond did a U-turn and we drove off. Robbie said his address and Raymond nodded. I looked gratefully at the back of his head. He was always helping us out. After we were burgled it was him who changed the locks and fixed the bolt on the back gate.

He turned the radio on. A song came on that I liked. I usually sang along to it. This time I sat quietly, holding my mum's hand. It felt like we were on the run.

EIGHT

Little Madden

The church was half empty. Terri looked carefully at the rows of people in front of her. She couldn't see him. A line of backs, some straight, some rounded, a couple sloped to one side. He usually sat near the front but today there was no sign of him. Her shoulders sagged with disappointment. Maybe he'd come late and was behind her somewhere. When the mass was over, when it was time to go, she might turn round and see his friendly face.

She stared at the altar. It was the young priest taking the mass, the one who tried to catch people's eye when he was doing the sermon. Trust her mother to want to be so close to the front. Terri glanced to her side. Her mother stood upright, her prayer book in her hand, her eyes fixed on the priest, her thumb automatically moving to turn a page.

Long fingers of sunlight poked through the high windows but they all seemed to fall around Terri, leaving her standing in the shade. The priest warbled on. Terri leant against the pew, longing for the moment when she would be able to sit down. Then she could meander around in her own thoughts.

She had a lot to think about. Her best friend's words played over in her head.

You're eighteen. You should be playing around with lads your own age, not falling in love with a twenty-eight-year-old man!

Terri closed her eyes and concentrated on the priest's voice. He was mumbling his words, saying the mass in a way that suggested he was in a hurry. That suited her. It wouldn't be much longer, five, maybe ten minutes. Then she'd be outside instead of being stuck inside this freezing church. She made a resolution. She would *never* force her children to go to mass.

She shivered, pulling the collar of her jacket up. She should have taken her mother's advice and worn her wool coat. She looked sideways. It was almost Easter and her mother was still wearing her scarf and hat.

The congregation mumbled something and Terri opened her mouth and closed it as if she was joining in.

Trish was always giving her advice. *You can't fall in love with Mr James.* But she had. Jon James, her English teacher.

He's old. He's your teacher. He's forbidden fruit. Face it, Terri, that's what you like about him. Nothing will happen between you and him. Doesn't that tell you something? You're afraid of boys and sex. That's why you've fallen for someone who is unattainable. That way you don't actually have to do anything.

Trish was always trying to analyse her. Just because she wouldn't open her arms to some sticky, smelly boy. Just because she wanted someone with a mind, a brain.

Mr James had seen every Shakespeare play there was to see. He wrote his own poems and sometimes used them with the class. He'd read all of Dostoyevsky's novels. Just last week he'd loaned her *Crime and Punishment*, his favourite book. She had it on her bedside table.

Mr James thinks of you as a little girl. Someone he teaches. He'd never do anything. He'd get sacked if he did.

Mr James used a fountain pen which he filled from a bottle of ink. The other kids laughed at this but Terri loved to watch as he did it. His fingers were delicate and his face had a look of concentration on it as he siphoned up the ink. His handwriting was small and uniform. He wrote whole paragraphs at the bottom of her essays that commented on her work. Words like *cogent* and *insightful* and *original* appeared along the margin. She read and re-read them, fizzing with pleasure at his words.

He's not even good looking, Trish had said.

She was wrong. He was tall and wore casual trousers and cotton jackets and open-necked shirts. She'd never seen him in a stuffy suit like the rest of the male teachers. And he carried his books and papers in a rucksack, not a briefcase.

He had sandy hair that flicked over his collar and a single gold ring in one ear. Terri's mouth went dry when she saw him. She longed to run her fingers through his hair and touch his face. Sometimes, in class, when he was reading a poem or a speech from Shakespeare, she imagined herself walking up to him, setting the book aside, putting her hand under his chin and tilting it upwards so that she could lean down and kiss him.

There was noise all around her. The congregation were standing up. The mass was almost over. Even her mother looked like she was winding up her prayers. One of Terri's legs felt like it had gone to sleep so she shook it and patted down her skirt. From behind she could hear the big church doors creaking as some people crept out early.

Moments later they walked out into the sun. Her mother immediately started talking to some people she knew so Terri left her and walked across to a bench and sat down. She looked around, her eyes jumping from face to face in the hope of seeing Mr James. If he was there she would go up to him and talk. She'd thought of things to say. She would remind him of a television programme on Charles Dickens that she'd noticed and then she would talk about the first couple of pages of *Crime and Punishment* that she'd struggled through the previous night. *Those Russian names are so difficult*, she'd say.

Mr James wasn't there, though. She sat and watched as the rest of the congregation emerged from the church. The sun slid in behind a cloud and the daylight changed from honey yellow to slate grey.

Her mother came walking towards her with a man and woman in tow. She huffed silently. She was always dredging up churchy people for her to meet. Behind them came two young children, a boy and a girl.

"This is Maggie Ryan and her husband, Steven. They teach at St Edward's Primary. Steven is a deputy head, and," her mum said, "he's a *writer*. He's been published as well."

"Hi," Terri said, smiling at the children.

"Not *published* as such," Steven Ryan said.

"Maggie is looking for a babysitter. I told her you had helped other people out."

"We'll pay, of course. It would be so nice to be able to go out now and then. What with work and the kids. We just don't seem to have any time to ourselves any more!"

The husband, Steven, was waving at someone across the way.

"Sure," Terri said.

"Maybe you'd give us your phone number?" Maggie said, pulling a notepad out of a big handbag.

Her mother said the number and Maggie Ryan wrote it down. Terri had one last look around the diminishing congregation. He absolutely, definitely hadn't come. She felt her jaw slacken and tried to smile at Maggie Ryan but her heart wasn't in it.

"Cheer up!" a male voice said.

She turned quickly, thinking the comment was for her. But Steven Ryan was picking up his little boy, who had just started to cry. Maggie turned away from Terri and her mother and spoke soothingly to the child.

After saying goodbye Terri walked off in the direction of home. She didn't bother to have one last look round. Mr James had not come to mass.

Turning into her street she saw her next-door neighbour, Jackie Gilbert, coming in the opposite direction. She was walking along with Kirk, her boyfriend. She felt her mother stiffen at her side.

"All right, Mrs P?" Kirk said, when they got closer.

"Fine," her mother said in a crisp voice.

"And the lovely Teresa?"

"Kirk!" Jackie said, giving him a shove. "Leave the kid alone."

Before Kirk came along her parents had done a lot for Jackie Gilbert and her three children. They'd babysat and shopped and did household jobs. They'd given her money and cooked food for them. They'd helped her claim the benefits she was entitled to and given her lifts here and there to hospital or doctor appointments. Her mother had even been a shoulder for Jackie to cry on when one of her children's dads was upsetting her.

One morning, when she and her mother were dropping some shopping off in the hallway, Kirk had appeared. He'd walked down the stairs behind Jackie in his boxer shorts and nothing else. He hadn't been embarrassed by their presence. He'd simply sidestepped them, lifted a carton of milk from one of the bags and walked towards the kitchen.

That had been five months before. Kirk was still around.

"Where are the children?" her mother said.

"We just popped out for a few minutes. Lizzie was asleep so we left Paul and Davey to look after her. We didn't want to disturb her."

Jackie's pregnant stomach protruded from beneath a cotton-top. Terri couldn't take her eyes off it.

"Maybe I'll come round later and take Lizzie out," Terri said.

"Any time. After lunch, maybe. Then I can have a little sleep. I get so tired."

"Not just a little *sleep*, darlin'," Kirk said, sliding his hand across Jackie's stomach, giving Terri and her mother a lascivious wink.

"Get off," Jackie said, smiling.

They walked round them and into their own house.

"Smell the alcohol?" her mother said, as they shut their own front door. "And they left two kids under six looking after a baby."

But Terri wasn't listening. The phone was ringing and she dashed up the hall to answer it. It was Trish.

"You'd better brace yourself," Trish said, sounding dramatic, "I've just heard something from Denise, whose next-door neighbour works in the school office. She overheard one of the deputy heads saying that Mr James has got a new job, starting after Easter. Guess where? In Scotland!"

Terri stared at the phone. Scotland?

"I phoned you as quick as I could. Turns out he was only temporary. This new job's permanent and it's in a private school. He's been given permission to go early. He goes on Wednesday."

Wednesday. That was the last day before Easter. The end of term. Only three days away. Mr James was going to Scotland. It seemed like the other side of the world.

"You're upset, aren't you? I knew you would be."

"I'm not. . ." she said.

"You must be. I know how you felt about him. Come round after lunch. We can talk about it."

"I can't. I've just said I'll look after Lizzie," she said.

"Bring her."

"Maybe."

Terri ended the call and walked up the stairs to her room. Her throat felt like it was all sharp edges and she swallowed a couple of times. Maybe it was for the best. Nothing was ever going to happen. Trish had said so.

There, on her bedside table, was *Crime and Punishment*. She picked it up and scanned the two pages that she had read the previous night. It had been hard to understand: too difficult for her, not something she would have chosen to look at. She took it across the room and pushed it into her school bag. She'd give it back to him. He could take it with him to *Scotland*. Maybe loan it to some other student.

She made a resolution. She would *never* fall in love with a teacher again. Never.

NINE

Terri eased Lizzie's pushchair up the incline. After a while she paused to get her breath. The woods were quiet and she was almost at the high point. Lizzie had fallen asleep, as she usually did whenever Terri took her out.

It was a Wednesday afternoon and she had no classes and no reason to hang around school. Mr James had been gone for over a month. Thirty-two days. She could probably give an estimate of the hours and minutes. School had once been a place she rushed to get to. Now the lessons seemed tedious; the work repetitive; the gossip dull.

She looked up, shielding her eyes from the sun. It wasn't far. In a while she'd be sitting down in the shade reading her book. If Lizzie woke up she'd take her out of the pushchair and let her have a toddle around on the grass. Lizzie liked that. She also liked to wander off into the bushes, so Terri would be careful to keep her close. She'd brought a ball and some skittles that they could play with. She edged the pushchair over some tree roots and back on to the main path.

Trish was free with her advice.

You need to go out with someone your own age. Unless you're afraid, that is. . .

Was Terri was *afraid* of boys her own age? It was not a word she would have used. Bored maybe, repelled sometimes, amused often.

She just couldn't take sixth-form boys seriously. They were physically big. They wore men's clothes. They had deep voices and facial hair and their shoulders were broad and their legs were muscular and strong. But inside they were still infantile. They were like puppy dogs. Playful and annoying at the same time. It was so easy to please them. A kiss, a hand on the breast, some heavy breathing and their tails started to wag. But Terri wasn't interested in just playing. She wanted something more, something big and huge and overpowering. Love. She knew it could never be with one of those boys. She'd known that the day that Mr James first walked into the classroom and read a Shakespeare sonnet to them. On that very first lesson he'd singled her out. *Teresa, what do you think Shakespeare is getting at when he says, "Shall I compare thee to a summer's day"?* She'd opened her mouth and stumbled out some words but her lips were dry as paper.

Now he was reading sonnets to girls in Scotland.

She got to the high point and sat down heavily on the trunk of a tree that had fallen and was slowly being eaten away. It felt dry under her legs, like a husk. She looked around. She hadn't come up this high for weeks. It felt fresher here, as if the breeze was skittering around on top of a blanket of heat. She looked around. The ground fell away on all sides and all she could see were trees or bushes. Not another person. Somewhere behind her was the road that led through the wood and eventually to Little Madden

Hall. The road was used by rangers or people who went fishing at the lake on the far side. She listened but couldn't hear a thing. Not a car or bike or human voice.

She was thirsty. She took her bottle of water out of the pouch at the back of the pushchair. Beside it was the bottle of baby juice that she'd bought for Lizzie. Jackie usually gave her a bottle that was half full of milk which warmed up and looked thick and made Terri's stomach turn. She always tipped it out at home, rinsed it and then filled it with juice. Lizzie liked it. She also took a disposable nappy from a packet she'd bought along with the juice. It meant that Lizzie was nice and dry and didn't smell bad.

Lizzie made a sound. She had woken up. Her cheeks were crimson from the heat. She held her arms out and Terri took a minute to unhook the straps and then picked the toddler out of the pushchair. She felt heavy, still full of sleep, her arms and legs hot to the touch. Lizzie wondered if she was just hot or getting a temperature. She sat her on the grass and pulled out the bottle of juice. Lizzie took it, tipping the bottle expertly and drinking the liquid.

Terri got the rest of the stuff out of her bag. The ball and skittles and some wet wipes that she used to cool Lizzie down a bit.

"Shall we play ball in a minute?" she said out loud, her voice sounding strange in the empty woods.

Lizzie followed Terri with her eyes, her lips sucking at the bottle, her cheeks ballooning. Her mother said that Lizzie was too old for a bottle, that she needed a beaker, but Jackie didn't have a baby beaker. Jackie didn't have much when it came to Lizzie. The toddler's clothes were shabby and her toys battered and dirty looking. Jackie often talked about a lack of money but Terri knew that she had loads of recently bought stuff for the new baby. Kirk's baby.

She noticed something on Lizzie's thigh. Three bruises. Each of them was the size of a five-pence piece, dark blue, almost black. They were centimetres apart and looked like pinches. Terri rubbed at them with her fingers. Lizzie gave a smile. She was such a good-natured baby, so pleased when anyone paid attention to her. The only person she didn't seem at ease with was Kirk.

Nobody was at ease with Kirk. Terri pictured him from earlier on when she'd picked up Lizzie. He'd come into the kitchen where she'd been with Jackie and the boys. He'd grunted at her and then stood half behind Jackie. While Jackie was talking he'd planted a wet kiss on her neck, his fingers playing with the straps of her top. All the while his eyes had been on Terri.

How different life was at the Ryans' house. Their children, so beautifully turned out, so well looked after, so cared for. What kind of lottery was it that threw some babies into horrible homes and others into caring, happy environments?

Not that the Ryans were perfect. Maggie was definitely overprotective of her children, fussing over their every move. When she was babysitting there was a piece of paper with phone numbers: the restaurant they were going to, her mum's, Steve's mum's, the doctor. There were also strict instructions on the bedtime ritual. Story at eight. Lights off at eight-thirty. Check on sleeping children every half hour.

As if she wouldn't have done it anyway.

Steve Ryan was more relaxed.

"Don't take too much notice of Maggie," he'd said, driving her home on the second or third time that she babysat. "She's a typical teacher. Trying to foresee every eventuality. Worry, worry, worry."

After that Steve gave her a secret wink when Maggie was reading the list out or rolled his eyes as they left and Maggie said, *Are you sure you'll be all right?*

Maggie's children were cosseted, whereas Lizzie. . .

Terri looked at Lizzie's arm again, the bruises were tiny but seemed deep. Had Kirk done this to her? Or one of her brothers? While Lizzie was drinking she examined the rest of her limbs but there was nothing else, no other signs of hurt that she could see. She'd tell her mother about it but she was always threatening to go up the street to Linda Harris, a social worker that she knew. *Leave it!* her father had said to her mother. *Live and let live.*

But her mother didn't want to leave it. She'd liked Jackie and the kids and when Kirk had come and changed everything she'd been upset and watchful and started to talk about reporting her to social services.

Lizzie had stopped drinking and was sitting up. Terri held the ball up and threw it gently into the air.

"Come on, Lizzie," she said, pulling the little girl's arm, "let's play a game."

Lizzie gave a banana grin and reached out to catch the ball.

TEN

The babysitting was good. The money was useful.

Terri had bought clothes and a Walkman and some tapes.

She was wearing her new jeans and strappy top. Her arms were bare and one or two people across the aisle had given her a funny look, as though she should have covered up for mass. She hoped none of them were friends of her mother.

She was at the back of the church. The service was almost over and she wondered who would be the first to creep out, pushing the creaky wooden doors open. Then she could go. Trish was waiting for her to come round so that they could revise together. The last exam was two days away, May 22nd. English Literature, Paper One, Shakespeare and Hardy. She'd learned the quotes, listed the themes, analysed the characters and the language. She was ready to go.

Trish needed help, though.

A couple of people in front of her made their way along the pew and walked to the back of the church. She heard the creak of the doors. In a few moments she would go as well.

A few rows ahead she saw a familiar shape. It was the back of Maggie Ryan's head. Her dark hair was pulled back into a green crocodile clip that matched her top. Steve was two seats away, the children in between. He was wearing a short-sleeved shirt and his neck jutted out of it, his dark hair cropped. He had his hands clasped behind him and Terri noticed he had his gold bracelet on. He didn't look like a deputy head. He looked too young, too muscular, too tanned.

At that very moment he turned and looked behind. His eye settled on Terri. He gave her a smile and pretended a yawn as if he was bored with the mass. She felt suddenly foolish, as if he'd known that she was looking at him, as if he'd felt her eyes on his back. She folded her arms across her chest and realized that the mass was finishing and she hadn't even left early.

She walked out with the rest of the congregation and waited. The Ryans came out laughing about something. Maggie waved at her and Steve gave a nod. She smiled as the children, Emily and Robbie, scurried across to her. Robbie had a badge on that said *I am Four!* They immediately began talking over each other, telling her about their trip to the zoo the previous day. When the Ryans reached her she straightened up.

"Terri," Maggie said, "how is the revision going?"

Maggie asked her this almost every time she saw her.

"Good. Last exam on Tuesday."

"How do you feel about babysitting tonight? If you're revising I can always ask someone else."

"Fine," she said.

"Are you sure? It's a bit last minute. Are you sure you haven't got a date?"

Steve was behind his wife and he rolled his eyes at Terri.

"No one goes on *dates* now, Mags."

"Whatever," Maggie said, sighing dramatically. "If you're sure you don't mind. I know you've done a lot for us lately."

"Honestly, no. Once the kids are in bed I can get on with some work."

"See you at seven, then," Maggie said, grabbing Emily's hand and walking off.

"See you then."

"I could show you that short story I'm working on," Steve said, touching her arm as he walked past, holding Robbie by the hand.

She nodded and watched him go.

She didn't mind babysitting. The money was useful.

ELEVEN

Grandad and her mother were having a row. She could hear their voices from the kitchen. It was probably about religion. Grandad was a lapsed Catholic and was always having a go at the church. Whenever he stayed little arguments sparked off. He had a booming voice and tried to drown out her mother's comments. Her mother was relentless, though, and always got the last word in, even as Grandad was on his way out, getting into his car.

She ignored them and thought about her exam, which was only a couple of days away. The last A level. Then she was finished for the summer. The long wait for the results and the preparations to go to Bristol. In September she would pack her boxes and go away from home for three years. Maybe she would move away after university, start a career, live in a flat; never come back to Little Madden to live.

She could always move to Whitby, where Grandad lived.

She walked over to her desk. On top of it was a short story. It had been neatly typed out on plain sheets of paper. On the front it said "The Affair" by Steven Ryan. She picked it up and flicked the pages. She'd read it three times so far. She put it down and covered it with some of her handouts.

She could see out into the garden. Some movement from next door made her shift closer to the window. Lizzie was out there. She was wearing a vest and nappy and shoes. She was toddling around, holding a purple stuffed toy that Terri couldn't quite make out. It made her smile. A new toy for Lizzie. She craned her neck to see if Jackie or any of the boys were in the garden but she couldn't see anyone.

The door of her room opened and she heard her mother's voice.

"Did you say you were babysitting tonight? Only I have some baby clothes for you to take. For Maggie."

"Maggie's pregnant?" Terri said sharply, twisting round.

"No! They're for someone she knows. Single mother, two kids, another on the way. No man, of course. In the past I'd have given them to Jackie. But not now. No, Maggie's not pregnant. I've no doubt she looks after herself. She'd probably call herself a modern Catholic. They listen to the Pope and then do their own thing."

She looks after herself. This was her mum's way of saying that Maggie used contraception even though the church didn't approve. Terri made herself look out of the window. She didn't want to think about the Ryans like that.

"All these modern women. I'd have given anything to have more children," her mum said in a wistful voice.

A shout from outside made her move to see what was happening. Kirk had appeared in the garden. He was striding towards Lizzie. Terri couldn't see the toddler's face but she heard her cry as Kirk snatched the purple toy from her and shouted, *That's not yours, you naughty girl! It's not yours. Don't take something that's not yours!*

"Oh!" Terri said.

She felt her mother at her shoulder, watching. Kirk stood towering over the toddler. His arm was tensing and for a horrible moment Terri thought he was going to hit the baby, but Jackie and the boys appeared and there seemed to be the beginnings of an argument. One of the boys ran towards Lizzie and hugged her.

"That family!" her mother said. "I am going to speak to Linda Harris. Your dad says I shouldn't interfere but. . ."

A noise from behind made them both turn around.

"He's right, you should mind your own business."

Grandad was standing in the doorway. He was using his fingers to roll up a cigarette.

"I'm just trying to be a good neighbour!" her mother said. "It's because of people like you that society's gone downhill!"

"People like me! What have I done?"

He put the cigarette in his mouth and started to sort through his pockets. In a second he pulled out a lighter.

"Godless people! People who have no moral code."

Her mother walked out, past Grandad. As she went he rolled his eyes.

"Hey, princess, you don't believe all this God shite, do you?"

Terri shrugged. She couldn't take sides, not when her mother was along the landing.

"I know one thing. Smoking is bad for your health."

"I'm sixty-five. I've never had a day's illness in my life."

"There's still plenty of time," she said.

She stepped across to him and made as if she was going to take the lit cigarette from his fingers. He put his hand up, though, mussing up her hair.

"Grandad!" she said, combing it back into place with her fingers.

He laughed loudly and went out of her room. She turned back and watched Lizzie playing with her brother. Her tears had gone and she was trying to kick a ball.

Terri looked at the clock. It was five-twenty. Two hours to go until she had to babysit. She should work, read over her notes. It was her last exam after all. Instead she pulled out the typed story. "The Affair". She lay down on her bed and began to read it again.

Terri didn't mind going upstairs, checking on the children, after they'd gone to sleep. That way she felt easy about going back downstairs and relaxing on the big settee, clicking the TV remote, watching the Ryans' huge TV. This evening she had had two glasses of wine. Maggie had pointed out the half-full bottle in the fridge. *Finish it off*, she'd said. *Steve'll drive you home so you don't have to worry.*

Emily was asleep on her stomach and Terri walked across and moved her hair back so that she could see the side of her face on the pillow, her mouth open slightly, breathing regularly. Robbie was on top of the covers flat on his back, one arm stretched up as though he were answering a question in class. The other was across his chest.

It was a hot night so she didn't bother to cover him up.

She walked back into the hall. It was almost eleven and the Ryans would be back soon. She was about to go downstairs when she saw that their bedroom door was open. She stepped towards it, giving the door a push so that it opened the whole way. She didn't turn the light on but she could tell that the bedroom was pale coloured. There was a wooden bed with a pastel-coloured duvet set. It was tidy, like everywhere else. She walked in. The only thing out of place was a discarded shirt on the bed. She picked it up. It was plain but looked expensive, like most of the things that Steve wore. She caught a faint whiff of aftershave from it and, pausing for a second, glancing towards the front window where the Ryans' car would pull up any moment, she lifted the shirt to her face and inhaled the scent.

On the way home she was silent. The wine and the heat had made her tired. Steve Ryan was taking his time. He was a careful driver.

"I liked the story," she said eventually.

"Did you?" he said, then paused. "I wrote it in two hours flat. Just thought of the idea and wrote it from beginning to end."

"It's good. You should try and get it published."

"It was you who gave me the idea," he said, pulling up at a pelican crossing.

She stared straight ahead. The red light burned in her vision. She felt him looking at her, his whole body turned towards her. She swallowed a couple of times.

"You should send it off," she said.

"I based the girl in the story on you," he said.

The lights changed and the car moved on, closer to her street, to her home. When he turned into the road they passed by her house and parked further up, five houses or so along. He pulled the handbrake and turned the ignition off. He didn't open the door, though, and she made no move to get out.

"I value your opinion," he said, "about my story."

"What about the novel? Are you still working on it?"

"Now and then. What with work and the kids, it's difficult to fit it in. A short story's easier, quick. You get all the practice with characters and plot and it only takes a fraction of the time. That reminds me, I've got something for you."

"For me?"

He reached across to the glove compartment, his arm brushing against her leg. He pulled out a paper bag and slid out a book.

"I found this in a second-hand book shop."

It was a copy of Shakespeare's sonnets.

"I know you said you liked a couple so I thought. . ."

"Thanks," she said.

She opened the book, letting the palm of her hand slide across the pages. He was leaning towards her, talking about finding the book, making his mind up about buying it. He'd had it for days, he said, but couldn't make up his mind whether to give it to her or not.

He was close to her. She could feel the heat off him, she could hear his breaths, she could smell his aftershave and shampoo and peppermint. She closed her eyes, her head light from the wine, dizzy with feeling.

"I should go," she said, her voice scratchy.

He pulled back to his side of the car and turned the ignition on. The car mumbled and she turned to go but at the last minute leaned across to his seat, her heart slowing down, almost stopping, and gave him a peck on the cheek.

"For the book," she said.

He gripped the steering wheel with both hands, his arms straight, as if he were clamping himself in place.

"See you soon," she said.

TWELVE

Jackie's front door was wide open so Terri went inside. She found Kirk in the living room sprawled out on the settee, a can of beer in hand. The curtains were drawn and the room was stiflingly hot. The boys were on the floor and they were all watching a loud film.

"What?" Kirk said, using the remote to pause the film.

"Where's Lizzie?"

"Upstairs with Mum," the oldest boy said.

"Shut the door!" Kirk said, starting the film, the sound blasting out of the television.

She went upstairs calling Jackie's name. At the top she saw Jackie's room door open and Jackie flat out on the bed sound asleep. She pushed the door of the children's room to get to Lizzie but it stayed shut.

She stepped back and looked up and down the door. It had a bolt on it. A brass bolt which locked the door from the outside. She frowned. She hadn't seen it before. It was crooked and looked like it had been put on by an amateur. She pulled it back and the door swung inwards.

Lizzie was lying in her cot, her legs in the air, a bottle hanging out of her mouth. Terri smiled at her and talked

77

in a baby voice as she plucked up the bottle. She looked with distaste at the soupy yellow milk.

"I've got a present for you," she whispered. "Come on, let's go for a walk."

Terri wheeled the pushchair out of Jackie's front gate and walked along in the direction of the wood. She thought about the bolt on the children's room door. It was a horrible thing to do. She would tell her mother when she got home. Maybe this time her mother would actually go to social services instead of talking about it all the time. Terri usually rolled her eyes at her mother's old-fashioned views of child rearing: _Those disposable nappies are so wasteful! Children should be in bed by eight. Only an hour of television a day._ But there were some things that just weren't right. Locking children in a room was wicked. If social services knew then that might force Jackie into looking after Lizzie better.

She made a resolution. She would _never_ be a single mother. She would look after herself like the _modern_ women her mum disapproved of. She would sign on at a new doctor's at Bristol and get herself some contraception. She'd have it ready even before she had a relationship with someone.

She would never be a single mother.

She sidestepped a couple of men carrying furniture out of a house further up. The woman who was moving emerged from her front door with a tray of drinks and the removal men stopped as soon as they saw her, one of them fanning himself with a T-shirt he'd taken off. Terri gave the woman a little wave. She hardly knew her, didn't even know her name but she was leaving to go somewhere else. It was only polite.

"Oh!"

She'd remembered something. She riffled in her bag, among the picnic things she'd brought, and pulled out the brand new Winnie the Pooh baby beaker. It was full of juice and she had some more in a plastic container.

"Here's your present," she said, taking the top off and handing it to Lizzie.

She replaced the top in her bag and her fingers caught the book she'd brought with her. She glanced down and saw the old-fashioned brown cover and the gold lettering, *Shakespeare's Sonnets*. It made her smile. She couldn't help it.

It was too hot to walk up to the high point in the woods so she took a different path around the perimeter, which would eventually lead her to the lake. It wasn't a route that she usually used but it was shady and pleasant and as she walked she felt a sudden feeling of freedom. She passed a couple of people walking dogs and a cyclist whose T-shirt was soaked in sweat.

The exams were over. Her schooldays were over.

There was still university to go to but the days of buttoning up her white blouse and knotting her tie were finished. It made her walk quicker, gave her a spring in her step. She was moving on, growing up, leaving home. She'd live in halls and mix with all sorts of people.

Trish approved of Terri leaving home.

You need to get away from your mum and dad and the church and that awful woman next door. You need to stand on your own two feet. University makes you grow up.

Trish wasn't going to university. She had a job in a building society.

I don't need to grow up. You're the one who has lived a sheltered life. No wonder you've never had a boyfriend. All that passion for Mr James. What a waste of energy! Anyway, Russell and me might get engaged at Christmas. It's a secret.

It wasn't a secret. Everyone knew. Trish seemed to have her life mapped out. Terri was different. She had no idea what she was going to do with her life. Her mother thought she'd be a teacher or a social worker. Something *vocational*. But she hankered after other things. A flat of her own, a car, an office job, where she had responsibilities, seniority. A job where she could dress up every day, go for expensive lunches, attend important functions. Then marriage and children? Like the Ryans?

She was slowing down. She'd been walking for over forty minutes. She'd find somewhere to sit soon. Then they could have their picnic and she could play with Lizzie.

She thought of the Ryans and the bottle of champagne that they had given her to celebrate the end of her exams. She'd taken it home in a bag and rushed up to her room without showing it to her mum. She placed the curvy bottle on her bedside cabinet. She'd felt over the gold paper at the top and wondered what it would be like to make the cork pop like she'd seen people do in television programmes.

The label had been written by Maggie. She had read it over and felt a stab of disappointment. Big strong letters that were neat and followed a straight line. Just like a primary school teacher. She had never seen Steve's handwriting. All of the things he had given her to read had been typed out. She imagined his writing as slanted, small, a bit like Mr James's.

He hadn't written the label but he had waited until Maggie was upstairs with the children and given her a peck on the cheek, whispering, *Well done you!*

She came to a stop. The path ahead widened out and ended at the road and the lake. It had no shade and the sun was fiery. She walked off the path through the trees, the pushchair bumping over the uneven ground. She could see a spot where there was some dappled sunlight and grass. When she got there she took an old towel out of her bag and spread it out.

She got Lizzie out of the pushchair. The toddler was damp with heat and perspiration. She lay her on the towel. Her nappy was soaked so she took a fresh one out of her bag and changed her. She put the dirty nappy in a plastic bag and tied it up tightly. She tucked it under a bush, intending to take it away with her later and put it in a bin.

She heard something. She listened for a moment but then Lizzie started to make sounds so she sat her up and sang a song. She clapped her hands in time with the beat and Lizzie tried to do the same. When she was finished she got a plastic box out of her bag and opened it. She took out a tiny square of sandwich and handed it to Lizzie.

The sound was there again. She looked around but could see nothing, just trees and bushes and sky.

She could definitely hear something. The slow crackle of branches and leaves mixed with a muffled tune, a pop song that she had heard over and over on the radio. She stood up, looking further, through the tree trunks, in the direction of the noise. She heard a loud creak, like a handbrake being pulled. There it was, further away than she'd thought, on the path that became a track.

A black car. It stood completely still, music coming from inside.

THIRTEEN

Epping

Mum was in a kind of shock. I held on to her elbow as she got out of Raymond's van, picking her way across his pipes and tools. Outside it was difficult to stand up straight. Raymond was brushing dust off Mum's shoulders. He looked as though he wanted to say something. He started a couple of times, *That mob . . .* and *I can't believe those people . . .* but then he seemed lost for words.

Robbie's mum, Silvie, burst out of her front door and walked smartly towards us.

"Come in, come in," she commanded.

Silvie was in her jeans and baggy T-shirt. There were paint marks on her clothes, brush strokes and splodges of colour. Her hair was cropped, like a man's haircut, and she had one feathery earring on.

Raymond stood at the door of his van.

"If you need any help. . ." he started.

He didn't finish because Silvie gathered Mum up and walked her towards the gate. Raymond gave me a look of confusion. He put his hand up his T-shirt and scratched his big tummy, then got back into the van. We trooped in behind Silvie and Mum. She took us into her long, thin kitchen, a place that I had sat with Robbie many times. We sat down and Mum lifted her bag on to the table and began to sort through for something.

"You can stay here as long as you like. And I don't need to know anything," Silvie said, holding her hands up in front of her to fend off information.

"There's nothing to hide," Mum said, moving things this way and that inside her bag. "Nothing at all. I haven't done anything. . ."

"You look like you need some brandy," Silvie said, and went out of the room, without waiting for an answer.

My mum finally found what she'd been looking for. Her mobile phone. She held it for a moment, her hand trembling. I wanted to reach out and steady her but she began to stab at it with her finger. Putting it to her ear she looked wildly around the room, avoiding eye contact with anyone. A few moments later Silvie appeared with a bottle of brandy and stood on a stool to reach for some glasses.

"Gerry? It's me. I'm not at home if you need to get in touch. There's some problems in the street and I'm sort of involved. Ring me on the mobile if you need to."

She placed the phone on the table, her shoulders dropping. She looked around. The room was long and dark, a galley kitchen. The walls were white and full of paintings by Silvie. Most of them were nudes. I'd got used to it over the months, male and female bodies in awkward positions, their flesh and parts on show. Mum seemed to notice suddenly, her eyes flicking from one to the other.

"Oh my," she said.

Silvie had a balloon-shaped glass nestling in the palm of

her hand. She poured the brandy in and handed it to my mum.

"You two clear off and me and Terri will have a chat."

I wanted to stay. I didn't like the idea of Silvie taking over Mum. But Robbie put his hand out and Mum was taking a long gulp of the brandy so I went upstairs.

"It's weird that she never told you the story until now."

Robbie was opening the window, pulling the curtains back to get some air in. I looked out. The rear gardens were short and backed on to other gardens. The houses across the way were close enough for me to see into the windows opposite. It was so different to my house. When I looked out the forest was there, shimmering in the morning sun or hunching against the rain or floating in the mist. My eyes were accustomed to a rippling expanse of green. Here it was brown creosote fences and red brick.

I flopped down on some of Robbie's floor cushions.

"Last night. After the police left. That's the first I've heard of it."

"She kept it a secret?"

"Not really. She didn't change her name or anything. She didn't try to hide away from it. She just didn't make an issue about it."

"You can stay here. We've got a spare room. You can stay for as long as you like."

I caught Robbie's eye. He looked *happy*. He had rescued me and Mum, and he had me there in his house. How could I back off from him, let him down gently, if he was in my face every second of the day? I felt miserable. I wanted to go home. To go back to our street. For things to be as they were. I didn't like the upheaval. I pictured Mum downstairs, drinking her way through the brandy, holding her mobile close in case Gerry Boyd rang her. And in our street Jade Henderson was still missing, taken from her cot in the middle of the night, carried out of the window and off through the garden into the forest. Somewhere else, back in time, another little girl had disappeared, snatched from her pushchair by a man in a black car. The two things were linked in people's minds. I had an image in my head. My mum, arms stretched out over eighteen years, holding each child by the hand.

Now they were both gone and we were stuck in the middle of a mess.

I wanted things to go back to the way they were. End of story.

Later that night a policewoman in plain clothes came. It was the same one who had called at our house two nights before. She was looking tired, her blonde hair a little flat on one side, as though she'd had a nap on it. We were all in the kitchen sitting with mugs of tea and a plate of sandwiches which Robbie had made. Sylvie had put some classical music on and it made the room seem very quiet, as if no one should speak too loudly.

"I'm Detective Paula Bramble. We've met before. Is there somewhere we can speak privately?" she said, her voice booming out.

Sylvie got up and gestured to Robbie. They left us in the kitchen, Paula Bramble scanning the walls, her face resting on nude after nude, her expression tight.

"Robbie's mum is an artist," I explained.

She nodded, then turned her eyes on Mum.

"Miss Parfitt, are you OK speaking about the arrangements in front of your daughter?"

My mum nodded. She was looking very small and hunched in Sylvie's big wooden chair. In front of her was a half-eaten sandwich.

"Do you mind if I sit down?" Paula Bramble said.

I pulled a chair out for her and she sat with a sigh.

"Is there any news about the baby?" my mum said.

Paula Bramble shook her head. She got a folder out of a bag and started to sort through it.

"Miss Parfitt, I've come to talk you through the next couple of days, maybe the next week or so. You'll know, from your experiences this afternoon, that feelings in the street are running high and I'm afraid that they are focusing on you."

"It's ridiculous," Mum said, in a whisper.

"Until there is some news on the disappearance of Jade Henderson we cannot guarantee your safety. It's our view that you and your daughter should stay in a safe house for the time being."

"You think someone will try to hurt us?"

"People are looking for someone to blame. A missing child – it's the worst thing. You'll know that."

"But it's nothing to do with me. It's not my fault. It wasn't my fault in Little Madden."

"There was no resolution then. People look at that with suspicion. Miss Parfitt, I'm not telling you anything you don't already know. You dealt with the public and the press twenty years ago. If anything it's worse now. The press are more intrusive, they whip up bad feeling."

"Do you think the baby will be found?" I said, interrupting.

"We are hopeful. We have no evidence that anything bad has happened."

Paula Bramble said these words slowly, as if she was tiptoeing round other words that she didn't want to say.

"Meanwhile, we have a safe house – a flat, actually – where you can stay until things are resolved."

"Why can't we stay here?" I said.

A couple of hours before I had wanted to be away from Robbie's house. Now that we might have to leave it felt comfortable, easy, homely.

"It won't take the press long to find you here. The young lad? Your boyfriend?"

She looked at me for confirmation and I nodded.

"They'll ask around, they'll find your daughter's school, they'll find someone to talk to. They'll be here in a day or so."

Mum stood up abruptly.

"You've made things clear. Do we have to go now?" she said, stepping across the room and picking up the bottle of brandy that Sylvie had left on the side. The balloon-shaped glass had been washed and was sitting upside down on the drainer.

"No. In the morning, at eight, there will be a press conference. I will take you to your home then and you can pack a bag maybe for a couple of weeks. Take enough stuff to see you through that time. We should be quick in order to escape any attention. Then I'll take you to the flat. It's not far and it's not a great flat but it'll give you a bit of breathing space."

Paula Bramble stood up. She combed her fingers through the limp side of her hair. She made it sound as though Mum and I were being pursued by a salivating mob.

"I'll see you in the morning, seven-thirty sharp?"

My mum had poured a large brandy out. She nodded, holding the glass by the stem.

"I went through all this twenty years ago."

"I'm sorry," Paula Bramble said. "We're trying to help you but you are not our priority at the moment. Jade Henderson is our number one. You're a mother. You can understand that."

Mum nodded. Then she lifted her glass and said, "*Cheers.*"

Paula Bramble's eyes met mine. There was a look of mild annoyance.

"Seven-thirty," she said and walked out of the room.

FOURTEEN

Mum went to bed in Robbie's spare room about ten. I dropped my bag on the floor as she pulled off her top and skirt and climbed into the double bed. By the time I'd gone into the bathroom, splashed my face and brushed my teeth, she was asleep. The third brandy had done its trick. She was lying with her back to me, covered with only a sheet, her chest rising and falling. I clicked off the light and went out on to the landing. Sylvie was downstairs but Robbie was in his room. I gave a light knock on the door and went in. He was at his computer filling in his blog. He did it every night without fail, had done for over a year.

"I won't be long," he said. "I brought up some wine. It's red, if that's all right."

I found red wine a bit harsh but I poured a glass out anyway and sat on the bed, my head against the headboard, kicking my shoes off and stretching my toes. I should have showered but felt too tired, too weary. At least Mum was asleep and I wouldn't have to worry about her crying or getting agitated or drinking herself senseless.

Robbie's back was straight. He typed with two fingers but rapidly, stopping every now and then to think or look at what he'd written. He called his blog *UndercoverDotCom*

90

because he wrote about everything that happened to him but never gave away the places or people he was talking about. There was a photo of him at the top but he was wearing dark glasses and had his hand over his mouth to cover his identity. When he described places in his life he put the initial letter. *My Alma Mater is KHS. Went to L. today. Walked to E. station. Sat for a while in L. shopping centre.* It was the same with people. He used their initials mostly: *Mr P, Ms CH, PMcT,* but some people had nicknames. I was *Miss Perfect,* which, in the beginning, Robbie assured me was to do with my surname being Parfitt. His mum was *Ms Van Gogh.*

It was one of the things that brought us together, his blog. The kids in class talked about it, looked at it when he first started. He was a funny, odd sort of boy and I was curious, so one night I went online and read for a couple of hours. I recognized lots of the school characters and situations he'd described. Some of the nicknames I'd worked out. There was a jokiness, a lightness to everything he wrote. He often put himself down, as if he didn't quite "get" what was going on around him. I scanned through again to see if there was any reference to *me*. We weren't close friends, but surely I was noticeable, *significant* in some way. But there was nothing.

The next day I went into school and sought him out. I told him I liked the blog but I was saddened to see that I wasn't in it. He shrugged. He was on his way to his class and I tagged along behind him trying to explain myself, but it was difficult. He was a lad I didn't know that well.

He dressed oddly and didn't bother with other kids much. I followed him along to his class and he stopped at the door.

"I go in here," he said.

"Right, see you later," I said, doing an about-turn and heading for my lesson feeling disgruntled, as if I'd made a bit of an idiot of myself.

That night I looked at the blog again.

Miss Perfect followed me today. She likes the blog but doesn't know why. She wants to be a character in my story. She enters at her own risk. I don't make friends easy and once I've made them I don't let go!

He called me Miss Perfect. It made me smile all evening. The next day I looked for him in the lunch room and sat down beside him. We talked, we waited for each other after school. We became mates. For months we were like best friends.

"Finished!" Robbie said, spinning round on his desk chair. "It's dramatic, I'll tell you that much."

He walked across to the bed. He sat down beside me, lifting his arm up to fit round my shoulders. I felt him playing with my hair and rubbing at my bare arm.

"Does everything have to go in that blog?"

"Not everything. But that stuff today, I can't leave that out. I've camouflaged it, though. You know I don't put personal stuff in, about us."

I nodded. It was true. He mentioned me from time to time but he hadn't charted the ups and downs of our relationship.

"You smell nice," he murmured.

I didn't. I needed a shower. I was hot, I was bothered, but it didn't seem to matter to him. He seemed to want me whatever I was like. I gave him a playful shove and moved over to the edge of the bed. He didn't follow me.

Best friends, we had been. If only I had left things like that. We went everywhere together. Our favourite place, since the spring, had been High Beach. It was a wide open space in Epping Forest with an old church and a pub and tea rooms. It was easy to get there, we just started from the path at the back of the gardens and snaked up through the forest for about forty minutes until we came to it. There were often lots of people and cars and bikes but it was big enough to wander off and find some private space. That was where I'd first kissed him. I stepped in front of him, put a hand on each side of his face, and pulled him down towards me for a long kiss. When I let go he seemed truly lost for words. The day after I looked at his blog and saw the words that pleased me. *Miss Perfect kissed me last night.* Later on was a cautionary note. *She does it at her own risk. I don't fall in love easily but I do fall in love for ever.*

Mum was snoring lightly when I got into bed. I lay down on my side. I closed my eyes for a few seconds but they opened again. The glass of red wine had not made me sleepy, even though I'd told Robbie it had. I was wide awake. I lay on my back and listened to the noises from outside: cars passing by, a squeal of brakes from a road that was further away. There were also footsteps from overhead, from Sylvie's studio in the loft. It was gone eleven but she was still up there working. Robbie said that she occasionally worked all night long and twice he had found her asleep on the cushions by her easel.

Mum sometimes worked late into the night, if she had a presentation to do or deadlines to meet. I thought of her at work. She always went dressed in smart clothes, her short hair neat, wearing subtle jewellery. I pictured her at the front door on her way out, faffing about with her briefcase, looking for last-minute things: her mobile, her discs, fruit lunch, her tiny umbrella that she often took just in case. She looked smart, not at all the way she looked when she went out with Gerry Boyd. Then she dressed down: jeans, trainers, brash jewellery, her hair spiky, high heels and maybe then she'd show the tattoo on her shoulder, the forget-me-not.

She was like two different people.

Now there was a third. A girl of eighteen, who had experienced things that I had never known about. Things she thought she'd left in the past but they'd turned up, like an unwelcome visitor, banging on the door, refusing to go away.

I leaned towards her and put my hand on her side. She was hot, her breaths coming slowly. I could fluff her hair up, I thought, but it wouldn't count because she would be asleep. I turned away and stared at the opposite wall. I could see the outline of one of Sylvie's paintings. *Man With A Book*. Naked.

It wasn't the first time I'd tried to sleep in that bed. I'd been there three weeks or so before when Sylvie was away and I stayed over. It was something I had looked forward to. A chance for Robbie and me to spend a whole night together. I closed my eyes thinking of it, trying to ignore the squirm of shame in my guts. For some reason Jack Slater came into my thoughts. I remembered him from earlier that day, on the tube, the girl with the boots hanging off his arm, whispering in his ear.

How different Robbie was to Jack Slater.

Jack Slater had been one of the most popular boys in school. He wore expensive clothes, had his hair in just the right style, was always carrying up-to-date CDs. He went to the fashionable pubs and clubs and was always turning up with different girls. Robbie was the opposite. I had liked the fact that he wouldn't wear trainers or any of the "sports" clothes that everyone else slavishly bought. He wore baggy jeans, cotton pants, leather brogues, old army shirts, second-hand stuff from Camden Market. I loved the fact that he sometimes wore bizarre badges. His favourite was one that said *I am Spartacus*. He rolled his eyes at the "clone" boys, as he called them.

His reluctance to get involved with me had been a challenge. Every kiss he gave me felt like forbidden fruit. I had to work at it. He'd wanted us to be friends. *I'm not sure I'm ready for a serious girlfriend*, he'd said. His words had spurred me on. He was something I had to *win*. And for those first few months it was a real talking point. People in school looked at us, they gossiped about us. I, who had never been particularly popular, was the source of much discussion. Neither Susie nor Grace could understand why I was with him. Even Jack Slater pulled me aside one day and asked me what I was doing with the geek. *When you could go for a walk in the forest with me,* he'd said, staring at me, his finger making circles on my wrist, sending a shiver up my arm.

I liked Robbie. He was bright and funny and caring and loyal. He was great company. He wasn't like the other lads. Five minutes' conversation with them usually resulted in a rough snog in a dark corner. Robbie didn't seem interested at all. He was happy to talk for hours and then just said, *See you!* and went off home.

The first time I kissed him he wrote about it on his blog and I waited, expecting him to come back for more, but he didn't. So I had to kiss him again and again and actually it became exciting to see if I could get a response from him. I did, of course. His eyes closed and his body tensed and he kissed me softly, his hand in my hair, for an age. When I stood up I was light-headed with desire. But he never pushed it any further. He never tried to unbutton my shirt or touch me. We were boyfriend and girlfriend. We kissed, we held hands, we went out together but we never *did* anything else. It meant that I walked around in a state of frustration: my chest aching, my skin crawling, my legs restless. When he said his mum was going away I suggested a night together.

I bought condoms. I bought wine. I lay in the bath for almost an hour. I dressed in my nicest underwear. I packed the wine and the condoms in my school rucksack. I sprayed myself with perfume, brushed my teeth and flossed them. In the mirror I checked my hair, I stood sideways, looking at the profile of my breasts. Would tonight be different? I wondered, using my hands to cup each breast. I took a deep breath and went to Robbie's.

He was doing his blog. He was wearing the same clothes as I'd seen him in earlier in the day. He looked momentarily surprised to see me, as if he'd forgotten I was coming. He gave me a hug and a kiss on the cheek. I showed him the wine and took my shoes off and sat on his bed.

We watched a DVD and had some pasta that his mum had made. Then we half sat, half lay on the bed listening to music.

I started things off. I kissed him and took his hand and placed it on my breast. He leaned back, puzzled, for a moment but then kissed me again and moved his hand so that it was under my top. I lay back and felt myself shiver at the feel of his skin on my skin. He helped me take my top off and we continued like that, moving around the bed. My eyes wanted to close, my chest and hips felt heavy and I kept wanting to push myself into him.

After a while I realized that was as much as we were going to do. If I wanted Robbie to do anything else I would have to lead him, push him on.

This is stupid, I thought.

I sat up, my lips feeling puffed up from all the kissing. I would have to move things on, *say something*. He leaned back on his elbow. He looked hot, his eyelids heavy. I was suddenly annoyed at him. Why didn't he take the lead? Why was he leaving it all up to me?

I pulled the condoms out of my rucksack.

"I bought these," I said.

He sat up. He coughed lightly, looking uncomfortable, as if I'd just produced a pornographic DVD for him to watch.

"Stel, I can't . . . I'm not good with . . . I've never done it before," he said, folding his arms across his chest.

"Neither have I!" I said. "Why don't we? Why not? We're together, aren't we?"

"I'd muck it up. I'm good with computers, not bodies. I'd do it wrong."

I couldn't believe what I was hearing. He was a boy. He knew what to do. All boys knew what to do. It came naturally, didn't it? I'd heard other girls talk. The most unlikely sixth formers seemed to have no trouble dropping their jeans and getting on with it.

"I've never done it either. We could learn together. All we have to do is get undressed, get into bed, see what happens."

It sounded so easy, so natural. In any case we were a couple, we liked each other. Wasn't that what couples did?

He went to the bathroom and I got undressed quickly and got into bed. I opened the packet of condoms and slid out one of the greasy rubber rings. I lay there waiting for him, feeling this tingle of excitement. I heard the bathroom door open and then Robbie appeared. He had undressed down to his boxers. His chest was white, his legs and arms thin. I was surprised. I had only ever seen him covered up with T-shirts and jumpers and jackets.

Then I looked down. His boxers had Daleks over them, all moving in different directions. He looked pathetic. He looked like a child. My eyes stayed on the garish boxers. I must have looked appalled.

"A present from an aunt," he shrugged, thinking it was the boxers alone that were upsetting me.

He stepped across to the bed and pulled the duvet back. I edged across to the far side of the mattress as he lay down and pulled the boxers off and flung them out of the bed. I pictured the Daleks spinning through the air and landing on the floorboards. I closed my eyes and felt Robbie move towards me. When his hand touched my skin I curled away, a feeling of nausea in my stomach.

"I can't!" I said, pulling at my clothes, which were on the floor. "I'm sorry, you were right and I was wrong. It's too soon."

I sat up and pulled on my pants and T-shirt and scooped up the other things from the floor. I stood up and looked back at the bed. Robbie looked mystified, hurt.

"It's my fault. I'm not ready, like you said. There'll be time, in the future."

I backed out of the room, sidestepping the Dalek boxers. I closed the door behind me and went into the spare room. It was too rushed, I said to myself. But later, when I was in the spare bed, deep under the duvet, listening for sounds from Robbie's room, I knew that it hadn't been too soon.

It had been too late for Robbie and me.

*

Mum gave a loud snore and turned in her sleep. She was at my back and I was still staring at the painting. *Man With A Book*. I felt her warmth and could still smell a hint of brandy from her. I reached back and took her hand, pulling it across me like we did when I was a child.

In those days I was the one who went to sleep first.

FIFTEEN

The street was quiet when we drove in. We'd only been gone for just over fourteen hours but it seemed like days. We came from the forest end so we didn't pass the Hendersons' house. When we pulled up in front of our house Mum gasped at the boards which had been nailed across the front-room window. At that moment Raymond came out of his house. He was wearing smart clothes for a change, trousers and a short-sleeved shirt. He looked more important than usual.

We got out of the car.

"You all right, Terri?" Raymond called. "And you, kid?"

Mum nodded. I shrugged. Could he not just call me *Stella*?

"I nailed the boards. I know a good glazier. I could get it done for you?"

"Would you?" Mum said. "We won't be around for a while."

"I'd leave the repairs for a few days," Paula Bramble said.

No one answered. We all knew what she meant. Don't replace the glass in case it gets smashed again.

"Where you going?" Mum called.

Paula Bramble was ushering us both up the path. She took Mum's keys and opened the door.

"See my bank manager," Raymond shouted as Paula closed the front door.

"We don't want to attract any unwanted attention," she said.

Mum went straight to the telephone and looked at the message button. It wasn't blinking. Gerry Boyd hadn't rung. She stood for a moment, licking her lips as if she was thirsty. Then she walked off into the kitchen and I heard the tap running.

Paula had dressed down. She was wearing jeans and a cotton top and was carrying a basket-weave bag instead of the leather holdall she had the previous night. I figured that she didn't want to stand out as a policewoman while taking us home and then on to the *safe flat*.

"We should be quick," she said. "Maybe fifteen minutes?"

Mum nodded. I went upstairs, into the spare bedroom, and took the two suitcases out from under the bed. I put one in Mum's room and then went into my own bedroom. I heard Mum come up a few minutes later.

It didn't take me long to pack. I shoved a bundle of clothes in, a coat and my ankle boots in case the weather turned. I sorted out a couple of books and my mobile phone charger. I tidied up my room a bit and found a small zip-up bag to put my toiletries in. For a second it felt as though I were packing for a holiday. Some holiday, I thought.

I couldn't hear much movement from Mum's room so I went in. She was sitting on the side of the bed. The suitcase was opened and there was underwear and a nightie and a couple of T-shirts.

"Come on," I said gently. "Won't you need some stuff for work?"

"I'm looking for my blue bracelet."

Paula appeared at the door, as if she'd been in the hallway all the time.

"Can I help?" she said, a hint of impatience in her voice.

"It's wooden. It's dark blue and it's got yellow flowers on it and I'm not going without it."

Paula sat down on the bed.

"Teresa, this might only be for a couple of days. Everything, all your stuff, will be here when you come back."

"I have earrings to match it," she said.

She opened her hand and showed a pair of dark-blue drop earrings with small yellow flowers, like daisies, painted on them.

"You'll find it. It'll be in a pocket somewhere, or a drawer. Thing is, Teresa, we don't have the time to look now."

Mum gave a dramatic sigh, reached across and laid the earrings on her bedside table. Then she stood up.

"Call me Terri," she said, "everyone does. Stel, can you sort this lot out for me? I need to go up to the loft. There are some photos and stuff I *have* to have with me."

She gave Paula a defiant look, as if daring her to speak, to forbid her from getting her photos. The policewoman just sat, neatly, on the bed. When Mum passed her she glanced at her watch and then stood up.

"I'll go down to the kitchen and empty the fridge of perishables."

I started opening drawers and cupboards and I took out items of clothes and toiletries I thought Mum would need. I grabbed her diary and some of her notebooks. From above, in the loft, I heard sounds of things being moved about.

As I went back into my room I saw Mum coming down the loft ladder. She was carrying a giant brown padded envelope. I gave her an encouraging smile. Then I dragged my case out of my room and edged it down the stairs. When I got to the bottom I stood and waited.

"Don't forget to lock up," Paula called upstairs, "windows especially."

It was an unnecessary reminder. After the burglary we were careful about locking up.

Moments later Mum started to come downstairs. Paula was shutting the kitchen door and holding a black plastic bag. I turned to the front door and noticed a card on the mat, as if it had been put through the letter box. I picked it up. On one side it had a line drawing of an old Victorian bathtub and the words, *Raymond Mann, Plumber*. A couple of phone numbers were underneath. I frowned. What was Raymond doing? I turned it over. There was a handwritten note: *If you need any help give me a call. RM.*

"What's that?" Paula said, looking suspicious.

"It's for Mum," I said, handing it to her. Mum read the words. Then she put the card in her jacket pocket.

"Let's go," Paula said. "If anyone is out there just put your head down and head for the car."

We went out slowly. I looked up and down the street. It was quiet. Like it used to be when I went off to school. Even the orange and green cable television van wasn't there. There was no one hanging round. I noticed a couple of extra cars parked around the Hendersons' but that was all. Paula put the black plastic bag in the wheelie bin. We walked across to her car and put our cases in the back. She was looking around, up and down the street, as if expecting a mob to appear from behind the hedge. I half expected her to speak into her watch strap like an American secret service agent. When we got into the car Mum seemed to wake up from the reverie she had fallen into.

"The press have gone. What does that mean?" she said.

"They'll be at the press conference," Paula said.

"But there's no one around. No one at all. It hardly seems worth us going anywhere," I said, looking wistfully back at my house, the wooden boards over the window looking crooked, as if they'd been nailed there in a great hurry.

We pulled away from the pavement and headed down the street past the Hendersons'. The house was shut up.

"It could mean that there have been developments."

"You mean they could have found the baby?" I said.

"Not necessarily."

"But that would mean we could stay at home. There would be no need for us to go."

"We think it would be better if we moved you. Just for a short while."

"But if they find the baby. . ." I said, my words fading at the end.

"They might find the baby dead, Stel. That's why we have to go. Isn't that right, Paula?"

My mum's voice was calm, matter of fact. Paula didn't answer but she nodded her head and we pulled out of Forest Lane and on to the high road.

SIXTEEN

The flat was ten minutes away. It was above a parade of shops in Debden close to the tube station. We had to go around the back and up a flight of iron steps. As soon as Paula opened the front door I could smell the stuffiness of the place. The walls were painted cream and the rooms were small and square. Two bedrooms, a living room, a kitchen and bathroom. Paula went round opening all the windows and telling us about the hot water and central heating. Not that we'd be needing the *heating*, she added quickly. They only expected us to stay for a week or two at the most.

Paula had a bag of groceries and she started to unpack them. She looked ill at ease and got in a muddle when she was showing me how to operate the cooker and the microwave. Then she put the kettle on.

My mum left her suitcase by the front door. She leaned against the kitchen door jamb clutching a holdall. I could see the brown padded envelope sticking out the top of it. She wasn't looking round, she wasn't interested in anything that Paula was saying. She looked tight, clamped up, her face flat and expressionless.

"This'll be OK, won't it, Mum?" I said.

She shook her head and turned away. A few moments later I heard a door close.

"Why don't you go and unpack. I'll talk to her," Paula said.

I shrugged. It was usually me who talked to Mum, who cheered her up if she was down, but this time I wasn't sure what I could say. I got my suitcase and took it into the small bedroom. I closed the door, wanting to cut myself off from the dismal situation. I lay the suitcase flat on the floor, unzipped it and lifted the lid. Should I unpack? I moved a few of my clothes about but left them there, in piles, in the case. I walked across to the window and pulled the net curtain back. Down below was the shopping parade, like an old-fashioned high street. There was a sweet shop, a baker's, a greengrocer's and a butcher's and a couple of charity shops. There were mostly mums and kids walking along, although a couple of young men were sitting, shirtless, on a low wall drinking beer. Behind them was an off-licence, *The Wine Barrel*.

There were some school kids standing outside the sweet shop wearing maroon uniforms and it reminded me, for the first time in days, of my own school. My lessons and exams were finished but the institution was still going on: the bells ringing, the kids jostling along the corridors, registers being taken, assemblies held, boys and girls whispering in corners. I still had a presence there; my name would be on teachers' registers. There would be a file that held my records, a library ticket of mine, a piece of work stapled to a noticeboard somewhere. My friends,

Susie, Grace and various others, would talk about me. Especially since the newspapers had written about Mum's past.

But I wasn't in school any more.

It gave me a funny feeling. I'd wanted to leave. I'd wanted to get a nice office job and be treated like an adult and yet I had this sudden feeling that I'd lost something.

I sighed and sat down on the bed. Maybe it was being there, in that colourless flat, that made me feel as if I were adrift. I lay back, my head hitting a flat pillow. I turned on my side and shut my eyes. What had happened to us? We'd been sucked deep into somebody else's troubles.

The Hendersons. People we didn't like.

I remembered Jade Henderson, on the passenger seat of her dad's car while he was struggling with wiring underneath the steering wheel. I'd been passing and stopped for a moment to look at her. She stared directly at me, her eyes big and curious. I made a little "boo" face at her and she smiled. I'd walked on but looked back a few steps later and she'd turned to watch me go and waved a "bye bye" wave, her hand up, the palm opening and closing. I did the same for a few moments until I felt silly and walked on home. When had that been? A week or two before?

What had happened to her? Who had taken her?

I heard a beep. It was loud and insistent. I went to my case and riffled among my things and pulled out my mobile. I turned it on and looked at it. There was a message. The name *Robbie* was on the screen. My teeth began to knock together. We'd only been apart a few hours and he was already ringing me.

I heard raised voices from next door and I went out into the hallway. The other bedroom door was half open. I heard Mum's voice, loud, strident, cracking in places.

"I just wish you people would be more honest with me. All this stuff about bringing us here to protect us – it's rubbish. You want me here to keep an eye on me because you think I had something to do with that little girl's disappearance."

"That's not true," Paula said, a hint of exasperation in her voice.

"No one believed me twenty years ago. Why should anyone believe me now?"

"This is silly, Terri. You're the one who's blowing this out of proportion. We've already interviewed you. You are here for one reason only. Your own safety. And Stella, of course. You don't want her frightened by that mob. You saw what it was like. Don't tell me you want to go back to that?"

There was quiet and I imagined Mum shaking her head.

"I'll come and see you every day and I'll keep you up to date on developments. As soon as this whole thing is concluded you'll be able to go back home."

The door opened. I didn't move away. I didn't mind that Paula saw me listening. The flat was too small for privacy and anyway I wanted to know what Mum was thinking, what she was feeling.

"Why don't you make the tea, Stella? The kettle must have boiled by now."

Mum stood up and lifted her bag from the floor.

"I'm going out to get a couple of things. That's allowed, isn't it?"

She sounded like a surly teenager. I backed off and went into the kitchen. As I was getting some mugs out I heard the door of the flat bang as Mum left. Paula was still in the hall, talking on her mobile. There were a lot of *ums*, so I couldn't make out what the conversation was about. I remembered the deserted street and wondered if the press conference had happened or if something more dramatic had happened, a discovery or an arrest. This gave me an odd curdling feeling in my stomach. Maybe a body had been found. It wasn't what I wanted to think about.

Paula was still talking but I'd stopped listening. I made myself concentrate on tidying away the remainder of the groceries and making the tea. My mobile was on the side and I picked it up a couple of times and thought about ringing Susie. I'd not been in touch much since my last exam. She and Grace were still in classes, preparing for year thirteen and university. Maybe I could call them, meet up somewhere, see what was happening at school, tell them what it was like to be under police protection. I shook my head. Robbie would laugh at that. *Police protection.* He'd probably write a blog post about it.

I could call him to let him know that we'd arrived safely. It was the sort of thing a friend would do. Keep him informed. When Robbie and I had just been friends we were on the phone a dozen times a day, chatting idly about work, music, television programmes. We talked about everything. That's how well we got on. Now, though, every call was weighted down with meaning. If I called him he would think I missed him as a *boyfriend*. He'd chat lightly, maybe make a joke but underneath his words I'd feel his longing for me like binds slipping round my wrists.

I needed him as a friend. But it wasn't possible to turn the clock back, to block out the previous months and just be mates again. I put my mobile down and started to pour boiling water on to the tea bags.

"There's been a development," Paula said, walking into the small kitchen.

I stopped what I was doing. I held my breath, expecting something awful.

"There's been a credible sighting of the baby. Three different people have rung the information line and reported a man and a baby on a caravan park outside Clacton. They reported it at different times, apparently, and all independently. The man arrived early yesterday morning and was seen trying to placate a toddler who seemed to be constantly upset. A policeman visited the site late last night but the man had left. There were indications of a quick exit. It could be significant."

"So Jade could be alive?" I said.

"Most certainly!" Paula said. "We are very hopeful. We have every expectation that this could have a good outcome. Most certainly."

Paula was smiling. Her shoulders were rippling and for a second I saw through all the police speak. She *was* hopeful. I felt my own chest relax and smiled as I heard the front door bang, keen for Paula to tell Mum the positive news.

Mum came into the kitchen holding a carrier bag across her chest. It had the words *The Wine Barrel* on it. As she lowered it to the table I heard the clink of glass. She pulled out three bottles of red wine, one after the other. I must have had a funny expression on my face because she pouted at me.

"What?" she said, looking from me to Paula. "I need something to keep me going, don't I?"

Mum pulled out a chair and sat down. Paula told her the news about the man at the caravan site. Mum listened quietly, her eyes on the three bottles of ruby-coloured liquid, dwarfing the mug of tea that I had poured. She picked up the tea and drank from it, the fingers of her free hand tracing the shape of the nearest bottle of wine. When Paula finished talking, she started to nod her head slowly.

"That's hopeful," she said.

There was quiet. Paula was looking at her mobile. Mum was looking at her mug of tea. I was picturing a little girl in a caravan. I saw her at a window, waving goodbye, her tiny palm opening and closing.

SEVENTEEN

Little Madden

The door of the black car opened and he got out. Music spilled into the woods, soft female voices singing in harmony. It was a song that Terri liked, a tune that often sounded inside her head. A love song. She'd hummed it for days when it was first released.

He stood by the door of the car. She was startled by the sight of him in the woods, the last place she had expected to see him. He was wearing casual clothes, jeans and a short-sleeved shirt. He looked unsure for a moment. Then he shrugged and raised his hand in a wave.

She smiled, the song surrounding her. The music seemed to fan out into the woods, incongruous and at the same time completely natural, as if it was a soundtrack.

Steve Ryan.

He leaned back into the car and turned the ignition off. The music stopped abruptly and the silence was blank, like an empty house. He pulled out a bottle of something and a red canvas bag and closed the door, the click sounding loud and out of place. Terri twisted round to see if Lizzie was all right. She was on her belly playing with some bricks, holding them up in the air.

"What are you doing here?" she said, shyly, when he was close enough to hear.

"Did I tell you I was going on a course today?"

She shook her head. She would have remembered.

"*How to Implement The National Curriculum.*"

She shrugged. It meant nothing to her.

"I was so bored. I almost fell asleep so I thought to hell with it. I'll go home, catch up on some marking." He stopped and looked down at Lizzie. "This must be your neighbour's baby. She's lovely," he said, dropping down on his knees in front of Lizzie. He laid the bottle down and put the bag on the grass. He picked up a couple of bricks and started to juggle with them. Lizzie followed his movements with her eyes.

"What's that for?" she said, pointing at the bottle lying on its side.

He stood up, grabbed the bottle and handed it to her. It was champagne. Ice cold.

"I brought it in the cooler box. Champagne has to be cold. I thought we could celebrate properly. The end of your exams, I mean. I've got some glasses and crisps and stuff. A sort of picnic."

"You've already given me a bottle. . ."

"This way I get to celebrate as well. You have to share the champagne with me."

"What about the conference?" she said, puzzled, not sure what was happening, why he was here.

"No one noticed me going. In any case I'd rather be here with you."

He brushed the grass off his jeans. He was staring at her for a moment as if he was considering something. Then he took the bottle of champagne out of her hand and leant down and kissed her. She stood rigid, her eye on Lizzie, her hands by her sides as his lips brushed back and forth across hers. The touch was light, like a feather. It only lasted seconds but it sent a flash of heat through her. Then he stood back as if he was waiting to see what she would do.

She mumbled something, turned away and squatted down to Lizzie. Her chest was tingling, her mouth ringing with the kiss. He had come for her. First the poems, then this. She straightened Lizzie's clothes and combed her fingers through the baby's hair. She couldn't turn back to look at him in case she swooned.

"How did you know where to find me?" she said, tidying up the bricks, her words croaky.

"Rang your home. Said I had a message from Mags. Your mum said you were out with the baby in the woods. I just took a chance that I'd find you."

She nodded. He took a chance. She stood up facing him again. He was being poetic. He was taking a *chance* on her, a gamble; playing with his life because of the way he felt about her. She put her hand out and touched his neck. He took it and pulled her towards him. She could feel his strength and the heat coming off him. She stared up at him, her eyes blurring at the closeness. He took her by the tops of her arms and pulled her tight to him, his mouth on her hair.

"I'll take a chance on you," she whispered, her face in his chest.

"Sure," he said, his voice husky, his hand slipping under her T-shirt.

They drank the champagne while playing with Lizzie. Steve pulled a picnic blanket out of his bag and laid it on the ground. Then he produced two champagne flutes and they opened the bottle. It didn't pop as Terri had hoped but the lid flipped off and the liquid fizzled up so that Steve had to pour it out quickly. They used the ball to play football and Lizzie toddled around, in and out of the sunlight, on and off the towel and the blanket as Terri and Steve shouted, "Goal!" After that they lined the skittles up, although Lizzie didn't really understand the game and wanted to throw them around. They piled the bricks up, building them into a tower and letting Lizzie knock them over. All the while Terri told Steve about Lizzie's family and about Kirk. Steve listened carefully, asking questions now and then. He told her about some cases of child neglect that he'd experienced. When she told him about the lock on the outside of the room door his face darkened. It wasn't right. He asked her if she wanted him to go and see Jackie Gilbert but she shook her head. She'd tell her mother and insist that she spoke to Linda Harris, the social worker. He shook his head. *If there was a fire . . .* he said and he looked genuinely concerned.

They were quiet for a while. The champagne was cold against her lips and tongue, the bubbles leaving a sweet taste in her mouth. Almost as soon as she'd drunk a couple of glasses she felt light-headed. It was past two and she hadn't eaten yet, her own sandwich sitting untouched in the plastic box next to the remainder of Lizzie's.

Steve was playing *Round and Round the Garden* with Lizzie. She watched as he took Lizzie's tiny hand in his and made circles on her palm with his finger. Lizzie's eyes were wide open and the anticipation showed gleefully on her face when his fingers crept up her arm to tickle her. As Terri watched a feeling of longing took hold of her, like a hunger. He turned and looked at her, his eyes flicking across her face and back to Lizzie. Even though he had his back to her she felt the air between them thicken.

Lizzie lay on her side on the towel, her thumb in her mouth, her eyelids hanging low, the sucking motion slowing down. In a few moments she was asleep.

Steve sat back beside her on the blanket. Without another word he pulled her towards him, kissing her mouth with urgency, pulling her shoulders into him, his hand dropping and lightly cupping her breast, his fingers hardly touching her. After some frantic kisses she pushed him back.

"The baby," she said.

He looked round. Lizzie was fast asleep. Her thumb had fallen out of her mouth but was still sticking up in a *thumbs-up* sign. Her face was relaxed, her mouth slightly open. Beside her, lying on the towel, was the Winnie the Pooh beaker that she had bought. She righted it.

"Let's just move away a bit," Steve said. "Just over there, by the tree."

"Not too far," Terri said.

Steve shook the blanket while Terri moved the pushchair close to Lizzie. She put the red bag on the other side in case Lizzie rolled over off the towel. The shade was heavy, there was no direct sunlight touching her. She walked away, ten, twelve paces, around the side of the tree. Sitting down she could see the edge of Lizzie's pushchair, the handles of the red bag. She listened for a moment. There were birds singing and the fluttering of wings amid the branches but nothing else. It was two-forty. In an hour the place would be dotted with school kids but now there was a soft quiet that she could just sink into. The champagne had made her feel dry-mouthed and she was about to say that when she felt herself being pulled gently from behind, Steve's hands under her top, stroking her skin. She lay back and then he was leaning over her, kissing her deeply, drinking her in. She closed her eyes as he pulled her close, his hands travelling the length of her back, her side, her leg. He hardly breathed as his mouth kissed her face, her neck, her breast.

"Wait," she whispered. "Wait, I can't . . . I don't . . . I haven't. . ."

"Ssh," he said, "I'm not going to *do* anything. I just want to touch you."

She lay back, her nerves fading. Out the corner of her eye she could see the pushchair and it registered with her that there was no sound coming from Lizzie. She felt herself sink into the grass as though it were a feather mattress. Opening her mouth she took his kisses, one by one.

Wasn't this what she had wanted?

After a while they lay side by side. She was on her back staring up at the sky. Her clothes were twisted under her. Steve was lying on his front, one arm across her. His shirt was out. *Enough!* he had said. *Enough, girl. I can't stand any more.* She had overwhelmed him. She raised her arm and looked at her watch. It was five past three. She thought there was a change in the woods, new sounds, cars along the lower road, some bikes nearby, somewhere, a distant call, a dog barking, maybe two. Soon the woods would be full of other sounds, children calling, bikes swishing past, an ice-cream van that stopped in one of the nearby lay-bys.

But not yet.

She closed her eyes. Just for a few seconds.

A noise jolted her awake. A shriek from somewhere high up. She looked up, licking her lips, her mouth parched. She couldn't see a thing. The sky was white, not blue any more. She lifted her head. It felt heavy with sleep. Steve was still beside her, his arm across her. She moved it and turned to the side. She looked at her watch. It was twenty-five past three. Twenty minutes had gone, swallowed up when she closed her eyes.

She sat up and looked around. The pushchair and the red bag were on the edge of her sight. She stretched her arms out and heard a mumbling from beside her as Steve was waking up. There, on the grass, by her foot, was the empty champagne bottle. She looked around. Something was different. Then she knew. The sun had gone in and there were no shadows. The grass looked dry and scruffy.

But that wasn't it. Something else was different and she couldn't put her finger on it. Something had changed, not just the colours, but the shape of what she could see.

The pushchair had moved. Or maybe, she thought, as she got on her knees and pushed herself up from the ground, maybe *she* had moved. In all the kissing and twisting and turning she and Steve and the blanket might well have travelled across the grass. She pushed herself up on her feet and stretched her arms. When she turned towards the baby an uncomfortable feeling took hold of her.

The pushchair was at a different angle to the canvas bag. It was.

She strode across the dry grass, a feeling of dread in her chest. The pushchair had been moved. But worse, much worse than that, the baby was gone.

"You all right?"

She heard Steve's voice from behind but she was like stone staring down at the towel on the ground, the plastic bricks strewn about, the football nearby. An empty space stared back at her. She stepped backwards away from it but the ground seemed to fall away beneath her feet. She staggered, feeling Steve at her shoulder.

The baby was gone.

"Oh no," he said.

The towel lay crumpled on the ground, just a small space, but its emptiness made it feel a gaping hole. She started to cry and then called out, *Lizzie, Lizzie, LIZZIE!* As if the baby might answer, might say, *I'm over here.* She walked around the towel, throwing the pushchair to one side, kicking the red bag. She picked it up, chucking it roughly into the bushes.

"Lizzie!" she shouted.

There was no answer. The woods were quiet.

EIGHTEEN

Steve took control. His voice was firm, like a straight line.

"She's probably woken up and crawled off," he said. "She may be nearby. We need to look, we need to do this in an organized way. Terri!" he said, gently shaking her by the shoulder. "Terri, we need to look for her *now*."

She nodded but her feet felt like they didn't belong to her. She went to move but nothing happened. She was stuck in one place, staring down at the spot where Lizzie had been lying, fast asleep, her thumb in the air, her beaker next to her. Now she had gone.

"Terri, you walk downwards towards the lake. Take single slow steps, looking around, calling her name. She can't have gone far. Look to the right and then the left before you take another step. Listen for any sound. She may have stumbled, fallen into some undergrowth. She might just be playing somewhere. We have to be thorough. We have to find her before. . ."

Before what?

Terri stared at him. He was walking up and down as he spoke. She could only see his profile, as if he didn't want to look her in the eye. He looked different now. The boyish stance was gone and he was round shouldered, his face drawn down, his chin squared with seriousness.

"We have to look. Now!" he said, giving her a little shove.

She started to walk, her head turning from side to side, her vision sweeping across the bushes and trees and undergrowth. In the distance she heard a bang which made her shoulders twitch. A car backfiring. That was all. She called the baby's name, her voice quivering. She looked deep into the woods for any sign of movement or colour. What had Lizzie been wearing? A white T-shirt? Not white, sort of creamy, and pink shorts, or had it been her blue ones? She had only ever seen Lizzie in these meagre clothes. Lizzie, who was pretty with wispy brown hair, who would have looked a treat in a dress or jeans and blouse. Poor baby, all she ever had to wear was washed-out clothes that had been bought from jumble sales, maybe even bought by her own mother. Charity for Jackie.

"Lizzie," she called, "Lizzie, where are you?"

She stood in an open area. The sun had gone but the clouds were bright white and the daylight hurt her eyes after being under the trees for so long. To the right was an area of long grass, the tips flowing backwards and forwards in the breeze. It looked like liquid, like water reeds.

A terrible thought came to her. The lake. Was it possible that a toddler could stumble down through the woods and get to the lake? No, no, it wasn't. It couldn't happen; Lizzie was only just walking properly, unaided. She fell over more than anything else, her sweet little face filled with confusion by the sudden upside-down world she was looking at.

The lake was only minutes away. She should go there, never mind what Steve said about searching slowly. If Lizzie was nearby she would have heard them, one of them would have seen her. But what if, by some strange fluke, she got as far as the lake? What then?

She made a sudden quick turn and headed back into the woods towards the lake. A wave of dizziness came over her and in her mouth she thought she could taste the champagne again, not cold and bubbly but warm and thick, like vomit. She didn't stop; she walked quickly at first and then began to run, leaping over branches and along the path towards the opening in the trees that led to the lake. It took seconds before she burst out of the woods and ran down the slope. She passed people and their dogs but she didn't stop, didn't ask for their help, she just careered down to the edge of the water.

It was quiet, barely a ripple breaking the surface. Where are you, Lizzie? she thought, gazing across the lake, the water almost black in the middle. Deeper than the rest, deep enough to suck down a small child.

She turned. What was she doing? Standing there imagining the worst when it was blatantly obvious that the baby hadn't come anywhere near here. She turned and walked rapidly up the incline and back into the woods. She should have stuck to Steve's plan. He knew what to do. He was responsible. He was a deputy head teacher. He was used to emergencies of one sort or another. Ten to one, ten to one he'd probably found Lizzie by now, just metres away, playing with some branches and leaves. He was probably playing *Round and Round the Garden* with her at that very minute while Terri was flouncing about dramatically at the edge of the lake.

She walked briskly, still looking round, her eyes hoping for a glimpse of cream, or pink; her ears tensing for the sound of laughter or crying. Not that Lizzie cried much, at least when she was with Terri. But alone in the woods, if she'd fallen and was hidden by some bushes she would be confused, fearful, she would wonder where Terri was, she might even call for her mummy.

It wouldn't take long to get back. Steve may well have found her and would be standing laughing, shrugging his shoulders. *What a drama!* he might say. Every step she took she forced herself to think this. The baby would be safe. The baby would be all right.

Up ahead she could see the place where she'd gone off the path, ages ago, when it had been too hot to push Lizzie any further. The sun had been blinding then but now it sat far behind the clouds. She stepped off the path. Further on through the bushes and trees she could see the shape of the black car parked on the edge of the lane. Hardly any cars came into the woods, just ranger's trucks and people with their fishing gear. She searched out the area round the car hoping for the sight of Steve holding Lizzie in his arms.

She closed her eyes and slowed down. Lizzie would be

there when she stepped into the clearing. Lizzie would be there. She walked on, her footsteps becoming heavy, the heat of the day pushing against her, like an invisible wall, holding her back. She could see the pushchair and the red bag and there was movement at the edge of her vision. It had to be Steve, it had to be him.

She stopped walking. There he was, bent over the blanket. Something sparked inside her. He had found Lizzie. He had laid her on the blanket for comfort. She tiptoed over, not wanted to break the quiet, to break the mood. But Steve turned, as if he had heard her. In his hand was the empty bottle and the blanket, folded up, ready to be put away.

No Lizzie.

He stood up and stared at her. His face was blank, his eyes stark. He shook his head. He hadn't found her. She felt herself crumpling up, her insides squeezed like an accordion. Then she fell on to her knees.

He was packing his stuff into the car.

"We have to get help," she said. "We can go in your car and ring the police, they'll know what to do."

He was quiet. He walked back to the pushchair and she followed him. He picked up the towel and the baby's things and put them in the pocket at the back.

"We need to ring the police!" she said, her voice louder.

He walked a couple of steps and picked up the football. He put it in the shelf under the seat of the pushchair. He knew, without looking, where everything went. He was a dad. He'd probably used pushchairs just like this when the children were young. She put her hand on his arm.

"What are we going to do?"

"I can't ring the police," he whispered, "I can't. I can't tell them I was here. You'll have to do it. You'll have to say you were on your own with the baby. I can't. . ."

She understood in a flash. She knew immediately what he meant. He couldn't admit to being *with her*.

"How can I?" she said. "I don't even know where a phone box is! You have the car. We can do it in minutes."

"They'll trace it. Someone will see me or you or the car. I can't be involved in this, Terri. There's Mags and the kids. And my job."

"The baby's gone missing. She might anywhere." Terri turned around, her arm flung out. "She might be hurt, she might even. . ."

She couldn't continue. What was she about to say? That Lizzie might be *dead*? Oh no, no. No, she wasn't going to say that because it wasn't true. Lizzie was somewhere, maybe nearby, lying on her back looking at the branches and the leaves. She was waiting for Terri.

"You need to go to the police," Steve said, taking her hand. "Take the pushchair, walk down through the woods. You'll pass other people. Tell them, ask them. Someone will be around. They'll drive you to the police station in the village."

"But you could take me. We'd be there in minutes."

"I can't. You must do it, Terri. Get started now. You're wasting time."

She looked straight at him. He was moving, imperceptibly, back towards his car. In a few moments he would be in it, reversing along the lane. She would hear the muffled sound of the music playing and he would give her a wave, leaving her to find the baby by herself.

"It's for the best," he whispered. "I'll go and you can follow."

She nodded. What kind of a man was he? How could he be thinking of himself when the baby was gone? Let him go. Let him get in his car and drive home to his wife and children. She turned away from him, choking back her feelings of anger, grabbing the handles of the pushchair, pulling it backwards towards the path.

"It's for the best," he called.

She didn't look at him. She pulled the pushchair roughly across the ground. It felt light, empty, unbalanced in some way. It needed to hold a baby for it to work properly. She got out on to the path and felt the sun on her back. She looked up at the sky. The clouds had parted and the sun stared pointedly down at her. In the distance she could hear the chimes of the ice-cream van. The afternoon had slid by. She walked along smartly, back the way she had come. How long would it take her? Thirty minutes? And then what? Straight to the police station? Or home to Jackie and Kirk and her mother? She stopped. What if she went back? Steve would be gone by now. What if she returned and looked again, carefully, under every bush, behind every fallen tree trunk, in among the long grass? What if she searched methodically? Maybe she would find Lizzie.

She turned the pushchair round and went back along the path.

At quarter to six she walked out of the wood, the pushchair still empty. She passed lots of people who must have wondered what she was doing. Maybe they thought she was a little strange in the head. She could have stopped, asked any of them for help but it was too late for that now.

Her feet were sore as she was walking towards the police station. Not a *police station* as such. It just looked like a house and had a policeman on duty during the day. She walked in and stood by a small counter. The policeman, a small thin man with half-moon glasses on the end of his nose, stopped what he was doing and looked at her expectantly. She must have been crying because he looked concerned and asked her if she was all right.

"I've lost a baby," she said.

She went on to explain about being in the woods, about playing with Lizzie, about the baby having vanished. After a few moments the policeman held his hand in front of her as if to stop her. He made her sit down and then made a number of phone calls, one after the other. Five, ten minutes later a man and a woman burst into the small reception and spoke to the policeman behind the counter.

"Have you got a search going?"

The policeman nodded.

The man and the woman took Terri into a room.

"I'm Detective Inspector Williams, this is Detective Cousins. We want you to start at the beginning," the man said.

She told them about going up to the woods with Lizzie, how she helped Jackie out by taking the baby off her hands, but the man seemed impatient.

"What happened to the baby?" he said. "This afternoon. You must tell me exactly what happened."

She remembered, sitting playing with her, giving her a sandwich and hearing the sound of the car pulling up. She stood up to see better through the foliage. There it was, incongruous, parked on the end of the lane but it looked as if it had been dropped in the middle of the trees. She remembered the door opening and the music wafting out into the wood. A love song.

"What happened to the baby? You must tell us!" the policewoman said.

She told her.

"A black car came and a man got out. He took Lizzie."

In a way, it was the truth.

NINETEEN

Epping

We spent a lot of the weekend in the safe flat. Mum slept most of Saturday morning while I read and watched the small television in the living room. A beep told me that I had a text. It was from Robbie. He suggested us meeting somewhere for a coffee. *I'll come in disguise*, he said and I couldn't help but smile. I opened a new text to reply but couldn't think of what to say. I didn't know if I wanted to meet him for a coffee so I put off sending anything until later. Hearing some movement from my mum's room I went in with a cup of tea. I saw that she'd shifted the bed so that it was close to the window. The chest of drawers was now on the opposite side. She hadn't unpacked but her work suit was on a hanger hooked on to the door of the wardrobe. She took the tea and patted the bed for me to sit down.

"Wait, I'll get my drink."

I carried my tea in and sat at the bottom of her bed, my feet tucked under her sheet, my toes resting on her warm foot. She stretched her arms up and then drank some of her tea. She always looked young when she was in bed. She wore an outsize T-shirt to sleep in and her hair was flat and her face scrubbed clean of make-up. She had no garish earrings in or necklaces, rings or bracelets.

"We haven't sat like this for ages!" she said, using her toes to tickle my feet.

It was true. Over the last few months I'd been busy revising and seeing Robbie. Even when I had the time I was worried that I'd go in and find Gerry Boyd's big face staring at me from Mum's pillow. So I usually got dressed and went downstairs, drunk my tea there and waited for Mum.

When we lived in Whitby, when I was much younger, I used to go into Mum's room at the weekends and get into bed with her. She had a rule that I couldn't go before eight so I'd often lie awake and stare at the clock as the minute hand crept slowly up to the hour. Then I'd jump up, run across the cold floor and race into her room. I'd pick up the corner of her duvet and slide myself in without even waking her. At my back I would feel the heat of her body and I used to reverse myself into the middle of her. All the time she seemed to be asleep and then, after I'd been lying in spoons with her for a while, she would speak, her voice crackly with tiredness, *Mummy needs to sleep for another five minutes, Stel. Just five minutes,* and I would lay wide awake staring at the wall, trying to work out in my head whether five minutes had passed.

When she woke we'd turn round and I'd be at her back with my small arm resting on her waist and we'd play games: *I Spy* or *What Would You Buy if You Won the Lottery?* Sometimes she'd tell me stories. More often she'd ask me to tell her stories and I went through my repertoire while she mumbled encouragement from time to time. Sometimes she fell asleep again and I had to give her a little nudge or a loud whisper in her ear, *Mum, it's time to wake up!*

As I got older the mornings changed. I began to sleep later so everything was rushed and there was no time for this. When I became a teenager I went into Mum's room at odd times of the day and sat on her bed so that we could chat. If I was cold I pulled the duvet up over my feet or legs.

The last time I sat on her bed was the day after Jade Henderson had disappeared, but that had been different. I'd been annoyed with her for staying out late without telling me. I hadn't been her daughter then, I'd been like a mum, moaning at her.

Today there was no duvet, just a white sheet.

"I wonder if there'll be any developments," I said.

"You sound like Inspector Bramble!"

Mum had started to call Paula, *Inspector.* Paula had corrected her a couple of times but then realized that Mum was doing it to be sarcastic.

"What do you think has happened to Jade Henderson?"

Mum's face disappeared behind her mug. A moment later she put it down on the chest of drawers.

"I'd like to think that there's a kind of innocent explanation but really, in my head, I know that some sick person has taken the baby."

"*Innocent explanation?*" I said. "Like what?"

"I don't know," she said, pulling the sheet so that it covered her shoulders. "There isn't one that I can think of, but. . ."

"What do you think happened to the baby that was taken from you?"

She threw the sheet back and lifted her legs off the bed. She stood up, stretching again, her T-shirt riding up so that her knickers were on show. She pulled one of the drawers open as if she was looking for something. It was empty and made a hollow sound as she shut it.

"I don't know what happened to Lizzie," she said quietly. "I told you that."

"But the man in the black car. What could he have wanted with a baby?"

She went over to her case and bent over, riffling through her clothes until she pulled out a pair of jeans.

"Do you know what, Stel?" she said, pulling them on, leg by leg. "It was so awful at the time – and since – that I just don't want to talk about it any more. I feel terrible for the Hendersons and dread to think about the little girl and what's happened to her but I'm trying to push it all away from myself, to pretend it's not really of any interest to me. Every time I do think about it the whole Lizzie business is dredged up and I feel like there's this great load on my back. I can't have that over again. Poor little girl, I hope more than anything that's she all right but really, it's not my responsibility. I have to distance myself from it. Otherwise I'll think too much about all this. . ."

Her hand swept the room. She meant having to move away from our home to the safe flat.

"I've lived in that street for nine years. Those people were my friends, my neighbours and look how they turned on me. They treated me like a dog – worse than a dog."

She was pulling an old blouse on, doing it up on the wrong button. I went to say something but it wasn't important. I shouldn't have brought the subject of Jade up. It was too upsetting for her. We were stuck in that grotty flat and we couldn't even talk about why.

She flopped down on the bed beside me and put her arm round my shoulder.

"Sorry, Stel, I'm not up to talking much."

"Let's not talk," I said, "let's play a game. What would you buy if you won the lottery?"

She managed a small smile and then lifted her hand and ruffled my hair.

Sunday crawled by slowly. It wasn't as hot as it had been but it was warm and there was a breeze that lifted the net curtain when I opened the bedroom window. I pulled a chair up and sat with my arms on the sill looking out at the parade of shops below. I must have looked odd, strange. I didn't care, though.

After what seemed like hours of sitting there I decided to do some housework. I found a small vacuum cleaner in the hall cupboard and began to vacuum the carpets. It made a noise like a juggernaut lorry but it didn't suck much stuff up. Still, I felt like I was doing something. It didn't stop me thinking about Jade Henderson.

Paula Bramble had been optimistic that she would be found. There'd been a sighting in a caravan park. It could all turn out right. Not everything in life was grim. There were happy stories. There were good people around. Just because some man had taken Jade away it didn't automatically mean that she wouldn't come back.

I said this to myself a couple of times as I slid the vacuum cleaner under my bed and then finally up and down the short hallway. Then I did the dishes and washed down the cooker. I even tidied the cupboards. It made the time pass quicker but it didn't stop me turning it all over in my mind.

A man took a toddler from her cot and carried her out of her house into the forest. Maybe he didn't go out the back window but crept through the house, out of the back door, through the garden and into the trees. Nearby, in a lane, he had an SUV. All the time the toddler was asleep. Possibly he laid her on the back seat of his car and covered her. He'd brought her monkey so that she had something familiar to hold, to smell. He took her on a drive, maybe to Clacton, to a caravan site.

Why did he do it?

After the housework was finished I tidied up my clothes, taking them out of my case, folding them neatly and placing them back in.

Don't talk to strangers, Mum had said, when I was growing up.

At the time I'd been confused. I talked to strangers all the time. My teacher was a stranger until I knew her. When new people moved into the street they were strangers. The man in the post office was a stranger. The lollipop lady was a stranger but I still talked to her. *That is not what I meant*, Mum had said crossly. *Complete strangers. Men.* But why? I'd ask over and over. Why? What will they do? My teacher, the policeman who came into school, Gloria from next door: all of them gave a similar response. They're dangerous. They want *to do things* to young children.

As a six-, seven-, eight-year-old I had no idea what they meant. Their faces simply folded up in front of my questions. They mumbled, they asked me to trust them, to believe that they knew better. When I was older, when I began to understand what these men did want, I was astonished. I couldn't believe it. I'd look at men, the shape of them, the size of them, their big hands and square jaws, their bellies and thick tree-trunk legs. Then I'd look at children, their small elf-like faces, their skinny bodies, their short legs and arms; their skin smooth like a blank page waiting to be written on.

Sometimes these men picked children up off the street, promising sweets or lifts home. Or they said they had a message from the child's parents, or that the child's dog was sick, or they claimed to be policemen who needed help or who had been sent by their parents to fetch them. The children who went with them weren't stupid. They were trusting. They hopped into the passenger seat of a car that took them on a journey from which they never returned.

I thought of Mum. An eighteen-year-old girl walking a baby in a pushchair through the woods. A man in a black car pushed her out of the way and took the little girl. What had happened to that baby? What had happened to Jade Henderson?

An insistent beep interrupted my thoughts. I was glad of it and I went round the flat looking for my mobile. I found it by the toaster. I looked at the screen. I sighed. It was Robbie again.

We could go and see a movie. Call me. Robbie.

I turned it off. I went and sat at my bedroom window and looked out at the shops below. There were kids of my age walking arm in arm with smiling faces one minute and shocked expressions the next. All the while their mouths were moving, bursting with chat and gossip and opinions. Sometimes they sauntered along. Then they would move quickly up to someone new and give a shriek and then a hug. Now and then they stopped, in the middle of the pavement, forcing people to walk around them. They looked so *alive*. I envied them. I was stuck in that tiny room one floor up, like a kind of prisoner. The only person who wanted to rescue me was someone I didn't want to see.

TWENTY

After the weekend Mum went to work. Her boss told her not to come into the office, as they were concerned that the press would find her there. Instead she was to visit a couple of corporate clients, big companies who donated to the charity. The first was in Essex and she spent a whole day there. The second was in South London.

"Stel, do you want to come with me? This place is in Blackheath. It's posh. We could have lunch in a pub."

She was getting ready, sorting her briefcase out. She had her suit on and for a moment looked pretty normal. Only the empty bottles of wine in the kitchen told a different story.

I shook my head. "I thought I might go shopping?"

"Please yourself."

Mum's voice was clipped, as though she was offended. I didn't think she really was, deep down. She went into the tiny kitchen and I followed her.

"I might go to the supermarket," I said. "We've not got much food."

She poured herself some orange juice and stood drinking it, her back to the fridge. I walked across to the sink and waited for her to answer. Since being in the flat we'd hardly sat down in the kitchen at all; rather, we'd eaten and drunk standing, as if we didn't want to get too comfortable.

"I s'pose so," she said. "Pasta, maybe, and some salad?"

I nodded. "I could take some washing to the launderette?"

She laughed. "You've never been to a launderette!"

"There's a first time for everything."

"Is there even an iron here?"

"I found one last night, in the hall cupboard."

She drank her juice and walked out to the hall.

"I'd better go. I've got a tube and a train to catch. See you tonight?"

I nodded.

She opened the front door and leaned across to kiss me.

"We'll get through this!" she said, and as she was moving away, out of the flat door, she gave me a lipstick kiss on my cheek.

"Oh, Mum!" I said.

When the door closed I grabbed a tissue and rubbed at my skin. Maybe it wouldn't be so bad, after all, I thought. Then I went into the bedrooms and collected washing and put it into a carrier bag.

The launderette was empty except for one man, sitting by the window reading a thick paperback book. He glanced up as I passed and I nodded. I had my pick of machines. I read the instructions and put some money in the powder dispenser before pulling the clothes out of the carrier bag.

I checked the pockets. Mum had a pound coin in her jeans. I tutted. She was always doing that. How often had I put a load of washing on only to hear it clinking round for the next hour and twenty minutes? I checked her back pockets and pulled out a plastic wallet, the kind that held an Oyster card. She had forgotten to take it with her. Now she would have to pay her fare to Blackheath. I put the wallet in the carrier bag.

I loaded the clothes into the machine and chose the cycle I wanted, fed the money in the slot and watched it start. The clothes moved in a circle and suds squirted across the glass.

The door of the launderette opened, letting in the noise of traffic. I turned to look and saw a familiar face. It was Jack Slater, the boy I'd seen on the tube a couple of days before. He was standing there with a dark-haired girl. My head sunk into my shoulders. I did not want anyone to see me. I stared at the washing machine and hoped he wouldn't notice.

"Hi!" he said.

I had to look round. He gave a smile. He was wearing shorts and a sleeveless T-shirt. The girl was wearing a short skirt and tight strappy top. He walked towards me. She followed him, swigging from a bottle of water.

"Stella Parfitt! That was you on the train the other day?" he said.

I nodded, wishing I were somewhere else. I wondered where the girl with the boots was. This girl had flip-flops on. She gave me a long-faced look. No doubt she wanted to be on her own with Jack. Neither of them had any washing that I could see.

"What you doing here?" he said, sitting down on the seat next to me. The girl sat further along, her bare legs stretched out, her toenails painted dark purple.

I pointed at the machine. "Washing clothes."

"No," he said, "I meant what you doing down here. Debden. You live in Epping?"

"Staying with a mate for a few days. I don't know if you've heard all the stuff about this toddler going missing in my street?"

"Yeah, I did," he said.

He was sitting close to me. When he moved his hand to pull his mobile out of his shorts pocket his arm brushed against mine.

"My mum had some trouble with the press," I said, not really knowing how much of the story to tell.

"I read about it," he said.

"Was that the baby that got abducted?" the girl said, leaning forward to have a good look at me.

I nodded.

"Bad situation," Jack said.

There was a quiet. The only noise was the washing machine. I looked and saw a muddle of mine and Mum's clothes twisting and turning in front of me. I wished they would go away so that I could be on my own. I could feel the girl moving around in her seat as if she wanted to go. I didn't know what to say.

"Just got back from uni," Jack said, breaking the silence.

"How was it?" I said, grateful for the change of subject.

"Great. It's good to be away from home. My parents are all right but it's much better to be on your own with no one looking over your shoulder. You applying?"

"No, I left school about a week ago. I'm getting a job."

He turned and looked at me, puzzled. I blinked a few times under his scrutiny. Then I looked away. The girl stood up, shaking her legs as if she were in an exercise class. Her breasts stood out of her T-shirt. I couldn't take my eyes off them. I imagined Jack Slater's hand reaching across to touch them and it gave me a weak feeling in my stomach.

"I thought you'd go to uni."

"No, I'm getting a job."

"We going, Jay?" the girl said, taking a couple of steps away from me as though to pull him in her wake.

"Coming," he said, without turning round. "You should go to uni. You'd enjoy it. Maybe come down to Brighton. See me. I'll show you round."

The girl was at the door.

"Well, I. . ."

He put his hand on top of mine and leaned over to my ear. I could feel his breath on my skin and it made my chest shiver.

"You can stay over in my room. I've got the space," he whispered.

He got up and walked away. When he got to the door he slid his arm around the girl's waist and gave her a kiss on the side of her head. When the door closed behind them I slumped into the seat, my ear still hot, my skin still tingling. Jack Slater was two-faced. Everybody knew that. Two different girls in the space of a few days and still he was giving me an invitation to come to Brighton.

I heard a beep and got my mobile out. It was Robbie again. I lay the mobile on the seat beside me and continued thinking about Jack Slater. He wasn't the sort of boy I would ever hook up with and yet there was *something* about him. Out of the blue I thought of Gerry Boyd. When Mum had first met him she said he *excited* her. She never knew what he was going to do, when he was going to turn up and whisk her off somewhere. He had ended up whisking someone else off and left Mum to find out for herself.

Robbie was so different, so dependable. I glanced sideways at my mobile. It lay in the middle of the seat, tiny and compact. In it was message after message; words of friendship, passion and maybe love. My feelings had changed, though. Now I just had to look at Jack Slater with a girl to experience a rush of desire. Jack Slater, narcissistic, self centred and heartless. Robbie, my best friend; loyal and caring.

I sat for a long while staring into the machine, my mobile at arm's length.

When the washing finished I folded it into a neat pile on the seat. I upended the carrier bag and frowned as Mum's Oyster card case tumbled out on to the floor. I fitted the bag over the washing, turned it back up the right way and then squatted down to reach for the Oyster card, which was on the floor. When I picked it up it was open flat in my hand. On one side was the card. On the other side was a photo of a girl.

I looked at it. It wasn't a picture of me but of a girl of about twelve. She was in uniform, some kind of posh school. It was maroon with a tartan pleated skirt. It looked old-fashioned. I wondered if it was Mum when she was a girl. She'd gone to a strict religious school. But it didn't look anything like Mum. The girl's hair was fair and her face was broad.

Who was it? I wondered.

I turned it over and there was a date. Just the year not the month or day. I calculated. The picture had been taken ten years before. Beside the numbers were two letters: EG. I smiled; e.g., *for example*. It wasn't that, though. It was someone's initials. The girl in the picture. Who was it? I thought. And why did Mum have it?

I put it in my jeans pocket and picked up the washing. Another thing to think about. As if I didn't have enough stuff on my mind. I scooped up my mobile and realized then that the man with the paperback book had gone. I walked to the door and stepped out in the street.

There, across the road, stepping off a bus, his Gap bag swinging untidily around, was Robbie.

TWENTY-ONE

We went to the café across the road. I tucked the washing under the table while Robbie went up to the counter. He was wearing a T-shirt that I hadn't seen before, deep blue; a colour that suited his fair looks. As he was queuing I looked him up and down. He was tall and thin and held himself straight. He had his money ready and had struck up a conversation with an ancient woman who was standing in front of him. He laughed at something she said. He was a nice person. Anybody would be lucky to have him as a boyfriend.

He'd left his Gap bag hanging over the back of the chair opposite. I noticed a badge pinned on to the strap that had the word *Badge* on it. It was the kind of quirky thing that would have amused me at one time.

I pulled out the Oyster card from my pocket and laid it on the table. I took the photo out and looked at it again. I had never seen this girl before. Her initials were there and the date, ten years before. She looked like a year seven, about eleven or twelve.

"How's it going?" Robbie said, interrupting my thoughts. "The safe flat?"

He placed two mugs of tea on the table and sat down.

"How did you find me?" I said.

"I rung your mum's mobile. You gave me her number once, remember? She told me where you were. Obviously I won't tell anyone else."

I took a drink of my tea. Mum probably thought that it would be good for me to have company. *Dependable, decent and clever. You should hold on to him!* she'd said. I looked up at him, across the table. I knew then, with certainty, that I didn't want him any more as a boyfriend.

"I've been calling you," he said brightly. "Is your mobile all right?"

I nodded. I wished we could go back to just being friends.

"Only I thought that, in the rush to pack, you might have forgotten your charger."

I shook my head.

"How come you didn't return my calls?" he said, looking puzzled.

"Thing is," I said.

He looked attentive. His eyebrows were slightly raised, as if he was waiting to see what I had to say. Then, in a instant, he seemed to know what was coming, his eyes looking down, his elbows resting on the table, his fingers cradling the mug.

"I'm sorry, Robbie," I said.

He looked up and I told him it was finished.

Afterwards, when Robbie's bus had come, I went to the supermarket for the shopping: pasta, tomato sauce, salad, bread and a bottle of water. I picked it all off the shelves dully. I paid for it silently, ignoring the cashier's attempts to chat. Then I went back to the flat, my arms hanging low from the weight of the bags. Once inside I slumped down at the kitchen table and felt the tears come. I'd wanted to end it. It was my choice. Still, for the second time in a couple of days, I felt like I'd lost something important.

Later I hung out the damp washing. I prepared a salad from the stuff I'd bought earlier. I sorted out the pasta and the sauce. The blue plastic wallet with the Oyster card sat in the middle of the kitchen table and it caught my eye as I moved round.

Something occurred to me. What if the Oyster card wasn't Mum's? What if she found it? Someone in the seat next to her might have stood up and rushed off the train and Mum might have looked down and seen the blue wallet too late to call out or give it back.

I snatched it up off the table and put it in my pocket again. It could have happened like that. A lost Oyster card. People were doing it all the time.

A couple of times, as I was passing, I leaned into Mum's room and looked at the padded envelope in her bag. I considered opening it. Then I backed out. Privacy: it was something Mum and I were keen on. She didn't nose around my stuff and I didn't interfere with hers. I did look at the photo again, particularly the date on the back. I went back into her room and did some mental arithmetic as I picked up the padded envelope and felt its contents. Then I replaced it.

A horrible feeling was settling inside me.

I sat down and turned the television on, waiting for Mum to come in from work. While the programme played on I thought of the initials. EG. The little girl who Mum had been looking after twenty years before. Her surname had been Gilbert and her first name was Lizzie. Elizabeth Gilbert. The date on the photo was from ten years before. The girl was eleven or twelve. Lizzie had been eighteen months old when she went missing.

Was this a picture of that girl?

I got up and turned the set off. I found myself walking up and down, peeking out of the window to see if Mum was coming along the road. I kept thinking that it couldn't be that little girl because Mum said she had been taken from her. Abducted. That was the truth of it. This photo, it was something else entirely. Or else it wasn't Mum's Oyster card. It was one that she'd found on the floor of the tube.

I heard the key in the front door and I walked out to the hall.

"What a day!" Mum said.

She threw her shoes off in the hallway and walked past me into the kitchen. She put her jacket round the back of a chair and went to the fridge, opened it and stood in front for a moment before pulling a bottle of drink out.

"I'm so hot!" she said.

"Good day?" I said.

"The tubes were all over the place and on top of that I forgot my Oyster card so I had to pay my fare!"

"Oh."

She went into the other room and I heard the sound of the TV. I stood for a while bursting with words that I wanted to say. Instead I made the pasta and sauce, put it on to a tray and carried it in to her.

"Thanks, love. I need this. Are you not eating?" she said, her feet stretched out along the tiny sofa.

"I ate something earlier," I said, and left her to it.

TWENTY-TWO

I went quietly into Mum's room and lifted the padded envelope from her case. I stood for a moment listening to the television from the next room. There was no sound of Mum moving so I slipped back into my own room and closed the door. I sat on the bed and looked at the envelope. It wasn't stuck down; it hadn't even been used. There was no address. It was just an envelope holding something.

I put my hand in and pulled out a wad of pages. They were held together by an old-fashioned bulldog clip. There was a note on top written in scruffy handwriting. *I collected these and kept them for you, Grandad.* They had been cut or torn from newspapers and were old. Their headlines and prints had faded and the white borders were almost yellow. I looked at the date on the top one and then those beneath: June, July, August, twenty years before. I read the headlines one by one, turning each page back like a notebook. Baby Abducted in Little Madden Wood; Babe in the Wood; Baby Kidnapped; Mystery of Missing Baby Elizabeth; Black Saloon Sought for Missing Lizzie; Local Girl Questioned Over Missing Baby; What Happened to Baby Lizzie? Police Digging Teams in Little Madden Wood; Hopes Fade for Baby Lizzie; Little Madden Wood Teenager Released.

I turned back to the beginning, skimming over the reports, mostly the first paragraphs. There were pictures too, of the woods, the village, the house where the baby had lived, of the baby herself. A small grainy shot of the baby's face. Chubby cheeks and a big smile. It looked like it had been cropped from a bigger picture, a group photo maybe. I flicked through to see if there was a photo of Mum but there wasn't. I laid them on the bed. Mum had told me the story but it felt uncomfortable to see it like this, like a running newsreel in my head.

There was one other thing in the envelope and I pulled it out. It was a plastic photograph album. It was small, the size of an address book, and had plastic pockets for each photo. I looked through. It wasn't full, I could see that. The first pocket was empty but after that there was one picture in each. They were all photos of the same girl, growing older. On the back of each one was a year. There were nine and the last one was dated this year. It showed a young woman in jeans and a baggy T-shirt. She was sitting on a swing in a garden, her arms around the ropes of the swing, clasped together in front of her. She had long fair hair and it sat on her shoulders. She had a pair of sunglasses back up on her head and she was smiling brightly. I felt in my pocket for the photo that I'd found in Mum's Oyster card wallet. I put them side by side. It was the same girl ten years apart. It was the same girl in all of them. These were photos of her growing up, through her teens, into young adulthood.

I slipped the missing photo back in the front pocket. Ten years of pictures. On the back of each were the initials

EG and the date. Elizabeth Gilbert. The baby who went missing. Here she was, alive and well, and Mum knew about it.

The doorbell rang. I still wasn't used to the odd sound of it and it startled me. I heard Mum's footsteps and quickly shoved the newspapers and photographs back into the envelope. Then I pushed it under the duvet. The door opened and I heard Paula Bramble's voice. I went out into the hallway.

Paula was wearing a dark suit. The look of her gave me a lurch in my stomach and I wondered if she'd come to tell us some bad news about Jade Henderson. I glanced back into my bedroom to make sure the envelope was hidden and then pulled the door shut.

"Come in, Inspector Bramble!" Mum said lightly.

Paula's expression didn't alter as she followed Mum into the living room. I went as well.

"Do you want a cup of tea?" I said.

Paula shook her head in such a way to suggest that a cup of tea was the *last* thing she wanted. Mum sat in an armchair, looking expectant. It only took her a second to register Paula's serious face, her formal clothes, standing in the centre of the room, stiff as a mannequin.

"Have you found the baby?" she said.

I had a strange moment. I imagined my mum when she was eighteen years old, sitting in a chair in the room of her grandad's house and asking that self-same question about Lizzie Gilbert. And yet why would she have asked it then? If she knew all along that the baby wasn't dead.

"No, no," Paula said, shaking her head. "The Clacton lead led to nothing. They found the man with the crying toddler further along the coast. He was an errant dad. Keeping his daughter a few days extra to spite his estranged wife."

"So it's back to square one. . ." my mum said.

"No, there's something else. It might be good if I could speak to you in private, Terri."

Paula looked apologetically at me.

"Why?" Mum said, sensing something. "What's up?"

"There's been an unexpected development."

"What?" Mum said. "What's it got to do with me?"

"I have to ask you, Terri, have you ever been in Jade Henderson's bedroom?"

"No!" Mum looked mystified.

"Are you absolutely sure?"

"I've never even been in the *house*. I don't know the family. I might have nodded to them if I passed them on the street but I've never had a conversation with any of them."

Paula's shoulders slumped and she looked like she could do with a sit-down.

"Officers made an inch by inch search of the bedroom Jade shared with her sister. They were looking for unusual things, things that didn't belong to the family. Mr and Mrs Henderson were with them. They were looking for clues, evidence. . ."

"So?" Mum said aggressively.

"They found a bracelet. The Hendersons say it definitely doesn't belong to anyone in the family, and they've never seen it before. It was in Jade's toy box, which Mrs Henderson says she had tidied up on the day of the abduction. She remembers because it was so hot and lots of Jade's toys were scattered about the garden. She said she felt a storm coming so she took them all in. She had to wash some of them so she cleared out the whole box. When the officers sorted through the box yesterday they found a bracelet. A blue wooden bracelet with yellow flowers painted on it. I saw it in the station. It's like the one that you were describing last week."

My mum gave a strange half-smile.

"I don't believe this. I had this twenty years ago. At least I was *with* the baby then. Now I'm being accused of taking a baby when I wasn't even there. I was at Gerry Boyd's house," she said, "I've told you that already."

"I'm just trying to make this easy for you. I didn't want the team to come here and arrest you. I asked them to let me bring you in."

"I was with Gerry Boyd!" she said.

"Until midnight. You said that in your statement but the baby could have been taken any time until two o'clock, when her father woke up."

"I was walking home. It was hot. Me and Gerry have been having some problems. I wanted to think about it."

"You said when we spoke first that you'd arrived home at one o'clock. Can anyone verify that?"

Mum looked straight at me. I knew what time she'd come in. It was after two. It had been raining and her clothes had been in a mess.

"It was just before one," I lied. "I know because I looked at the clock when I heard the front door slam."

Paula nodded.

"The bracelet is a problem. Terri, you'll have to come down to the station and talk to the team about it."

"But what can I tell them? It's not a designer piece of jewellery. I can't even remember where I bought it. Some chain store probably. Anyone could have bought an identical one."

Paula was shaking her head.

"We checked. It's handmade, from a shop in Brighton. They made a hundred or so of them a couple of years ago."

Mum rolled her eyes. The bracelet had been bought in Brighton. I remembered the day. We'd been out with a man she'd been seeing for a few months called Eddie. He'd bought her the jewellery and me a little wooden beach hut painted red and white. He was nice but she broke up with him a couple of weeks later.

"This is madness. I've done nothing!"

"Come down to the station with me. If there's an explanation we'll find it."

My mum stood up.

"Give me a minute," she said and walked towards the bedroom. I followed her. She picked her bag up and pulled out her mobile phone.

"I'll come to the station with you," I said.

She shook her head and put her hand out to ward me off. I felt stung. I felt angry. Why did she want to keep me out of it? Was she afraid that I'd find out something else?

"You didn't get home that night until after two!" I whispered.

She looked at me with a sort of hopelessness. Why wouldn't she just open up to me?

"We should go," Paula said from the hallway.

"This is history repeating itself," my mum said, shaking her head.

She gave me a fierce hug, her thin arms holding me tight. Her mouth was at my ear and she whispered, "I did walk home from Gerry's. Somewhere along the way I must have sat down on a bench. I was so drunk I fell asleep. I never told you because I was ashamed."

She let go of me and fiddled about with some shoes. Then she walked out of the bedroom and followed Paula out of the flat. When the door shut I felt this swooning feeling and went into my tiny bedroom and across to the window. Down below in the street was Paula Bramble's car. My mum was walking towards it. She looked smaller than usual. She still had her work clothes on but the shoes were flat backless sandals and beside Paula she looked like a little girl. I felt this twinge in my chest and pictured her, asleep on a bench in the middle of the night like a drunk.

It was as if she was someone different, someone I didn't really know. Her bracelet was in Jade Henderson's bedroom. She had photos of Lizzie Gilbert even though she said Lizzie had been snatched from her.

I didn't understand any of it. End of story.

TWENTY-THREE

Little Madden

A lot can change in ten years. A new housing estate had been built on the other side of Little Madden Wood. Terri took a walk through it, pausing to look at the tasteful detached houses that backed on to the dense trees of the old wood. There were ten, each in a different style, all with two or more cars parked in drives or outside. How different to the street she grew up in, on the other side of the village. The houses, tightly packed together, hardly enough room for cars to park, the neighbours within reaching distance.

Then there was the supermarket and DIY store that had opened on the outskirts of the village. She'd stopped there, that morning, on her way. She'd seen a handful of the people she'd known at school. The biggest surprise was seeing Trish, standing by a display of double glazing, giving out leaflets. *It's just part time. Gets us a bit of holiday money. With three kids we need every penny. Great to see you, come round and visit, see Russell and the girls.*

She'd nodded but she wouldn't visit Trish. She hadn't come back to Little Madden to renew old friendships. She'd come back for the remembrance service. Ten years had passed since the day Lizzie Gilbert was taken. Terri remembered it as though it were yesterday, herself stumbling out of the woods pushing an empty pushchair, heading for the police house, trying to find someone to help her.

She'd noticed, when walking through the village, that the police house was no longer there. It had been closed, along with the post office and the grocer's, years before when her mum and dad were still living in Little Madden. The police house was now privately owned; the forecourt where parking was allowed had been turned into a front garden.

The place had changed. There were speed humps in the streets and hanging baskets everywhere, colourful flowers tumbling out of them. There was a tiny pedestrian square in the centre next to the old village green. It had benches and a small play area for children. It was perfect for a seven-year-old like Stella. But she hadn't brought her daughter. Stella had never visited the place where she grew up. Her parents had moved away and there had been no need to visit Little Madden in order to let Stella see her grandparents.

As she walked towards the church the place felt unfamiliar, as though it were some other village that she had wandered into. It was hardly surprising. In the last ten years she'd only been back once, to move all of her stuff out of her parents' house. She had hoped never to return.

But this one last time was for Lizzie.

After it happened she'd stayed with her grandad, in Whitby. She'd hidden there, away from the press and away from Jackie Gilbert and Kirk, both of whom had publicly threatened her. Grandad had welcomed her with open arms, believed her completely, calling her his *princess*. He swore at the police when they came to talk to her. She'd heard him on the telephone having arguments with her mother and father, telling them that the whole story was total *shite*. She'd watched from the upstairs window as he stormed out of his house into the street where a couple of journalists had parked their cars. The next day he'd paid for a solicitor to try to get an injunction preventing the press from coming near her.

He couldn't stop the police from coming, though. They came every day at first, mostly Inspector Williams. They went over and over her story. Before leaving Little Madden she'd taken them to a place in the woods where she said it had happened. It was somewhere she and Lizzie had visited in previous weeks but it wasn't where Steve had found her; it wasn't the place where they'd drunk champagne and fallen asleep. It wasn't the place where Lizzie had been taken from. She was afraid the police would find some evidence of her and Steve together and know she was lying. The police scoured the place and didn't find a thing. They interviewed everyone who had been in the woods that day. One or two thought they'd noticed a black car moving through but most people said they hadn't seen anything. Some remembered her. A girl, pushing an empty pushchair, her mouth moving as though she was talking to herself. Eventually the police widened their search and they found the plastic bag with Lizzie's nappy in it. They came to Whitby for her and drove her all the way to the wood, the car speeding along the country roads as though they'd been chasing some criminal. She was a liar, they said. This was where she'd been with the baby. She said she'd got mixed up, she apologized, she cried, she appealed for them to believe her. She had nothing to do with Lizzie's disappearance. How could they believe her, they said, when she'd deliberately lied to them?

In Whitby she went to a phone box and rang Steve Ryan's school. She needed his help, she said, she needed him to tell them the truth. He'd spoken to her softly. He reassured her, told her that they would leave her alone if she just bided her time. What was the point of dragging him into it? Wouldn't that just distract the police? Send them on a false trail? And how would it help get the baby back? She heard a bell ringing from his school. He had to go, he said, he knew that she'd do the right thing, not for him but for the baby.

She stayed in her grandad's house as the investigation continued. She thought of Lizzie. Someone had taken her when she and Steve were asleep. Who? Why? Where was she now? These were questions she couldn't answer but they were on the tip of her tongue for days, weeks, months, until the end of September when the police stopped ringing or calling, when it was time for her to go to university, when the newspapers had tired of the story.

Lizzie Gilbert was gone. Lost to everyone who knew her.

*

The tiny church was only half full. In the front row Terri could see the back of Jackie Gilbert's head. Alongside her were her children, one of the boys taller than she was and then others in descending order. Her mother told her that Jackie and Kirk had got married a couple of months after Lizzie's disappearance. There had been problems, though, with the new baby, and it and the other two kids were taken into care. Jackie had stuck with Kirk for a couple of months but then he'd been sent to prison and she'd got together with a man who ran a pub in a nearby village. She eventually had another baby. She got her two boys back but Kirk's baby stayed in long-term foster care. After that Jackie's life continued to be up and down.

The three rows behind Jackie were full up but the rest of the seats were largely empty. Terri was right at the back, in the corner. Not because she was afraid to face Jackie. Rather, she didn't want to associate with them. All of the neighbours, the friends – they'd all believed that she had had something to do with Lizzie's disappearance. Even after the police had publicly stated that there wasn't a scrap of evidence to support this, they had still mumbled about there being *no smoke without fire*. Her mother had told her all of it, in long phone calls to Whitby. Even ten years later, Terri had no reason to smile or be friendly with any of them.

The service started and there were hymns and prayers, most of which Terri ignored. How different it was to a Catholic mass, the atmosphere lighter somehow, as if they were all in a meeting rather than a religious service. When the sermon came on she closed her eyes and remembered Lizzie and her chubby cheeks, her happy smile. She pictured her lying on the blanket as she fixed the pushchair on one side and Steve's red holdall on the other; in case Lizzie *rolled in her sleep*. She remembered the special beaker she'd bought her and the games they'd played with the skittles. She even managed to visualize Lizzie's face, but the image was dappled and wouldn't stay still long enough for her to look closely, to remember the little girl as she was. Then it slipped away completely and she opened her eyes, aware that one or two of the people in front had noticed her presence.

Along the pew she saw that she'd been joined by another woman. She looked at her for a moment, wondering who she was and why she had come into the service late. The woman was older, maybe forty-five, and she was wearing a dark-coloured mac even though it was warm outside and there was no hint of rain. Terri looked back up to the front of the church and saw that Jackie Gilbert had turned round and was staring at her. Terri kept her expression still. She wasn't going to smile or show in any way that she was affected by Jackie Gilbert's glare.

Terri bowed her head. The woman along the way had knelt down and was looking at the order of service sheet. Terri picked hers up and read through it.

A service to the memory of Elizabeth Gilbert
Who went missing ten years ago in Little Madden Wood.
Never to be forgotten.

She felt her throat tighten. She had never forgotten Lizzie and never would. Did that make up for the fact that she had taken her eye off the little girl, long enough for somebody to bundle her away in the back of a car? It must have been a car, mustn't it? How else could a man conceal a small child and smuggle her out of her community? Or was she thinking this to excuse the fact that she had told the police a lie, that a man in a black car had stolen the baby from her? Had she told this story so often that she had ended up believing it?

She held her eyelids tightly shut. She did not want anyone to see her crying. After a few moments she heard a murmuring noise and she was reminded of those days when she used to go to mass and pass the time by losing herself in her own thoughts. It was only the noise of people moving, whispering, that alerted her to the fact that mass was over.

She looked up. The vicar was at the front talking to Jackie and other people. She turned to go and noticed that the older woman in the mac had gone. She edged along the pew and walked out of the church into the bright sunlight. Her car was parked on the edge of the village and she had a sudden sense of panic that she should get off quickly, get to her car, before anybody came out of the church. As she walked she opened her bag and sorted through for her keys but she was ham-fisted and couldn't find them, eventually fishing them out only to drop them on the ground.

She heard the noise of people coming behind her and

was about to walk off when she felt a hand on her shoulder. She turned round to see Jackie Gilbert standing, white-faced, in front of her.

"You took my baby. You did something to her. I know you did. The police know it. Just because they couldn't prove it doesn't mean that they don't think that. I hope you rot in hell. I hope you never have kids, I hope you're infertile because they'd never be safe with. . ."

Terri was silent, standing under the onslaught. Jackie didn't know that she already had a daughter. Why should she? She let her speak on, her words ugly and spiteful. Perhaps she deserved it. A man stepped in front of Jackie.

"She's not worth it, Jackie. Leave it. Not today. Not on your daughter's special day."

Jackie's face was rigid. She looked like she was about to say something else and then she stopped, her shoulders falling, her face breaking into lines, her eyes narrowing as if she was about to cry.

It's not my fault, Terri wanted to say; she wanted to shout it out but she didn't. She turned and walked away, along the street with car humps, past the closed shops and the police house that was no more. She put her head down and threw one foot after the other until she turned out of the main street towards the tiny car park that said *Pay and Display*.

There were cars parked around hers and she had the key ready in case others were following from the church. She saw the woman in the mac standing by a red car. She looked at Terri as if she'd been waiting for her. Terri opened her car door. She didn't want any more conversations. Maybe it had been a bad idea to come but she'd done it for Lizzie.

"Excuse me," a voice said. "You're Teresa Parfitt?"

The woman was standing in front of her car as if blocking her way. What was she? A journalist? That was all Terri needed. She didn't answer. She got into the car and turned the ignition. When the woman stood her ground she opened the window and called out.

"Excuse me!" she said.

The woman came to the window.

"Will you just look at this?" she said, handing a small brown envelope in to Terri. It hung in mid-air between them.

"What is it?" Terri said, annoyed, glancing to the side of the woman in case any of the others from the church came round the corner.

"Just look at it. There's a telephone number on the back. If you want to talk about it you could ring me."

Terri stared at the envelope, angry now. Why couldn't people leave her alone? She half thought she'd drive off, leave the woman standing with her stupid envelope. She took it, closed the window, waited for the woman to step back and drove off.

Once she was out of the village she kept driving, all the way to her parents' house. Stella was there and she was longing to see her, to hug her, to play games with her. Stella would want to know where she had been. She'd tell her she'd been to see a long-lost friend, which in a way was true.

Ten minutes later, she pulled into a space outside the house. She saw the envelope and sighed. More relaxed now, she picked it up and tore the top open. If the woman had been a journalist and this was some offer for her story then Terri would tear this letter into a hundred pieces.

But there was no letter. Just a photograph. A picture of Lizzie.

Her mouth went dry looking at it. Lizzie, not as she knew her, not as an eighteen-month-old toddler, but older, maybe two or three, playing in a sand castle. Her face was thinner, she was taller, she was standing up like a proper little person. It was Lizzie, though, she was sure. It was. She turned it over. There was a date. The year after Lizzie went missing. There was a handwritten message and a phone number.

If you want to talk about this ring me. Margaret Sloane.

TWENTY-FOUR

She arranged to meet Margaret Sloane that afternoon in the garden of the Tudor Hotel in Printon, a small village ten minutes' drive from her parents' house. Her phone call to the woman was brief, icy. She was angry and couldn't wait to let the woman know exactly how she felt.

Her first look at the photo had given her a jolt, made her sit in the car for ages before going into the house. She'd stared at it until it seemed to recede in front of her eyes. But in the hour or so since she first saw it she had become unsure. The face was too thin, the smile not quite right. She thought of the woman in the church wearing a long mac as if to hide herself away. Maybe she was a journalist and she was trying to get Terri's attention. What better way than to give her a photo of Lizzie? It was most likely a fake. She'd heard of new computers that could alter images and she decided that this woman was working for some newspaper that wanted a story on the tenth anniversary of Lizzie's disappearance.

It had to be so because if the picture was *real* the alternative was unthinkable. Lizzie had been taken and *murdered*. This was the truth of it. The police hadn't said it, the newspapers hadn't said it but that was what they all thought, that was what everyone thought, even Jackie Gilbert.

That's why she was going to meet this odd woman. To put her in her place. To sort out whatever scam she was planning.

Stella was helping her gran and grandad. Terri watched as her daughter and her mother made fairy cakes for the church fête the next day. Her father was down at the end of the garden collecting the strawberries. Terri remembered the process well. The little bun cases, with pleated edges that had to be separated and lined up side by side. The mixture, scooped up on a dessert spoon, edged into the cases with the aid of a teaspoon. The smell of the buns as they came out of the oven. When she was a child it had been all she could do not to grab a couple and run up to her room and eat them. *Honestly*, her mother would say, *it's for charity*. Then there would be the whipped cream, a dollop on each and a strawberry that had been halved and placed on top like tiny wings.

The process hadn't changed and Stella was standing in front of a row of fairy cakes, each of which was having cream spooned on to it in readiness for the strawberries. Her daughter looked as though she was salivating. Terri walked across, picked up her denim jacket from the back of the chair, put her hand out and mussed up Stella's hair.

"Oh Mum!" Stella said, patting it down.

"I'll just be an hour and then Stella and me will have to

make tracks," she said, ducking back so that Stella couldn't do the same to her.

"You don't have to go back tonight?" her mother said.

"I told Grandad we would. He's organizing the tea."

Her mother nodded stiffly. Any mention of Grandad brought a dark look to her face. It was her opinion that Grandad had lured Terri away from them, away from the Catholic church. It hadn't been like that, though. Grandad was the only person who hadn't doubted her. Never. Not once. That's why, after university, when she found out she was pregnant, she'd gone to Whitby. He'd looked after her without judging. He'd left her to look after her baby without interfering. He'd helped her to get a job and live a good life, at first with him but then in flat round the corner where she and Stella could be a tiny family.

"I suppose it was his idea for you to go back to Little Madden," her mother said.

Out of the corner of her eye she could see her father coming up the garden with a bowl of strawberries. She opened her mouth to say something, to put her mother straight but then she looked at Stella and knew it would upset her if they argued.

"I must go," she said, "I'll be half an hour or so. Maybe not even that long."

Her father was at the French doors. She reached out and took one of the fairy cakes, plucked a strawberry from the bowl and went out of the kitchen, ignoring the protests from behind her.

*

Margaret Sloane was in the hotel garden already. Her red car was in the car park and Terri parked alongside it. She'd taken off her mac and was wearing a short-sleeved white blouse over some black trousers. She fitted in with the kind of people sitting in the garden, formally dressed even though it was a hot afternoon. She had both hands around a tall glass of something. Terri saw that her nails were manicured, a light shade of pink, hardly noticeable against the pale skin of her hands.

She sat down opposite.

"Would you like something?"

Terri shook her head, took out the photo and placed it on the table between them. Margaret Sloane frowned and covered it with her hand, looking round.

"I've come here to talk about this," Terri said.

"Of course," Margaret said.

"Are you a journalist?"

Margaret gave a slight smile, hardly moving her lips. "No."

"This is a fake. I think you're trying to get me to talk about this, to give you information so that you can write it up in a story and put it in your paper. You people make me sick. I never did anything to that baby. She was taken from me. You people, you journalists, you made me out to be a monster."

Terri's voice had got louder and one or two people were looking round

"I'm not a journalist." Margaret Sloane said it quietly, leaning down to get something out of her bag. Another

172

envelope appeared. A bigger one. Terri gave it a suspicious look.

"I'm not staying. . ." she said, determined not to be pulled into a conversation.

"I have some more photos of . . . of Lizzie here. You can look at them if you like. They're genuine. Every one of them."

She began to open the envelope and Terri stood up. This is what journalists were like. They tricked people. This woman was trying to get her to talk about that day in the woods and she was doing it in this underhand way. Like a magician, trying to distract her with a sleight of hand.

"I didn't do anything wrong. I told the police everything," Terri said, standing still, looking from the envelope to Margaret Sloane and back again.

"I know you didn't do anything wrong," Margaret Sloane said. "I was there that day. I saw you. I know what happened to the baby."

Terri shook her head. This was priceless. The newspapers would try anything.

"You don't know," she said. "Nobody knows."

"I know that you were asleep and you were with a man," Margaret Sloane said.

Terri's legs felt like clay. She held on to the edge of the table and looked at the woman sitting down, her nails perfectly curved, her face carefully made up, her hair cut and styled. She couldn't speak, she couldn't think, she couldn't move.

"Why don't you sit down, Teresa. We can talk without drawing too much attention to ourselves."

"No," she said, shaking her head.

She had to get away from this woman, this person who had just lifted a lid on something that was private, secret, her business. She felt her car keys in her hand. Why was she still standing there when she could be driving away, along the lanes, back to Stella?

"Sit down, Teresa," Margaret Sloane said. "There are things you need to know about Lizzie."

Terri sat down. She positioned herself neatly on the chair, her knees together, her elbows at her ribs. Inside she was ready to burst.

"I had hoped we could talk," Margaret said, "but deep down I suppose I knew that we wouldn't be able to. That's why I've written this." She indicated the envelope. "It explains everything. It'll take you half an hour to read it. That's if you want to. If you don't want to look at it then there's a rubbish bin in the car park."

She offered the envelope. Terri turned her head away.

"I'll leave it here, on the table."

Terri could hear Margaret Sloane getting up and the sound of her heels as she walked away. She turned and watched as the woman went into the back entrance of the hotel. Then she sat staring at the envelope. Looking round the garden she saw people in twos and fours sitting smiling and laughing, lifting glasses up to their mouths, gesticulating with their hands, whispering in each other's ears. In the distance she could hear some music, a pop song coming from inside the hotel.

She looked up at the windows and wondered which of

the rooms Margaret Sloane was in. Was she, at that moment, standing beside a curtain, looking out to see if Terri took the envelope?

Terri sighed, reached across and grabbed the edge of it and pulled it towards her, until it was on her lap.

Then she opened it.

TWENTY-FIVE

She read the letter quickly the first time, hardly believing the words on the page. The second time she did it with more care, her eyes following the words slowly, reading them and rereading them until she got to the last page.

Dear Teresa,

I know so much about you. I know that people call you Terri but I'm not sure I dare to be so familiar. You are twenty-eight. You are not married. You have one daughter and live in a flat in Whitby. You work in the offices of a children's charity. I know these things because I've made it my business to find out.

Today was only the second time I had ever seen you. You were smaller than I expected, younger looking, just a teenager really.

The first time I saw you you really were a teenager, lying on a blanket in Little Madden Wood, a man at your side. But I'm getting ahead of myself. If you've decided to read this then I need to tell you my whole story.

I am Margaret Sloane. I am forty-seven now and have lived in Scotland for ten years with my daughter, Emily, who is almost twelve. I am a wildlife photographer. A freelance.

I take pictures of flora, fauna, insect or animal life and sell them to publishers. They're used in textbooks or magazines or calendars. It's a labour of love.

This was what I was doing, on that day, ten years ago in Little Madden Wood. Taking photographs of birds. But I'm going too fast, leaving bits out, and you need to know the whole truth about me.

I was married to a university lecturer. We were together for eight years. The first five years were wonderful. I built up a reputation for some fine work and my pictures appeared in journals and magazines all over the world. That's the beauty of wildlife photography, there are no borders. A picture of a robin nesting can be enjoyed in Japan or Ecuador. I was successful. Not rich or well known, you understand. But among my peers, in my field, I had high standing. After five years of marriage we tried to have a baby. I was not so successful there. We tried IVF. We had to pay a lot of money and after a further three years and three attempts I still couldn't conceive. By this time the marriage was falling apart and then one day, my husband told me he had met someone else. It was a recent thing, he said, a sudden passionate affair that was completely beyond his control. To my shame I followed him to the flat of this woman and watched as he went in. I saw a glimpse of her face at the door. She was young, maybe in her twenties, possibly a student. I stood on the corner watching the front door determined to confront them when they emerged. I waited for what seemed like hours until it finally opened and they came out hand in hand. I was trembling with emotion, ready to walk across and confront them.

But my legs became heavy and immobile when I saw her. She was pregnant, her bulge obvious under a tight pink T-shirt. The marriage was over. I moved out of our home, shook off all the social ties I had had as part of a couple and went to visit my mother and father, who had moved to France some years before.

Imagine my astonishment when during that stay I found out that I was pregnant. It was my husband's baby. In the middle of the emotional upset I had stopped bothering about menstrual cycles and dates. I started feeling queasy a lot of the time, my breasts became heavier, my waist was thickening. I told no one. I came back to England and rented a flat in the Lake District as far away from him as I could. I did some freelance work with lake fowl and water reeds. I looked after myself: no drinking, no smoking, early nights, good food. I decorated a nursery. Then, when the baby was born, I was happier than I ever thought I could be.

But this story has an unhappy ending, you'll have realized that.

Her name was Emily and she died when she was fifteen months old. I went into her room one morning as I usually did. I looked in her cot and she was lying on her back. I started to talk to her in that silly way that mothers do. I opened the blinds and turned round. She wasn't moving. It was Sudden Infant Death Syndrome, otherwise known as cot death.

Why am I telling you this torturous story? To gain your sympathy? To get you to like me? So that when I tell you the rest you won't think so badly of me? Maybe I just want you to know my history. Our actions are not always spur of the moment things. Sometimes they grow from deep roots, long-buried desires.

There I was, thirty-five years old, sitting on the floor next to my baby's cot waiting for the ambulance men to come and take her away. Would you like to hold her one more time? they said and I shook my head. I did not want to feel how cold or stiff she was.

For months after this I wandered up and down the country, taking pictures, staying at short-term lets. I bought a camper van and went abroad, I travelled through Europe. I took many pictures, not just wildlife. I was attracted by bright colours, red in particular, and as I travelled I found myself taking shots of men, women and children in red; red curtains, red flags, red cars. Everything in a rich blood red. The colour of life. And then one day I sat on a bench by a road in Croatia and watched the cars tearing by and I knew I wanted to go home.

I rented a cottage in a remote part of Scotland. I wanted to start again, to make new friends, build up my work. I decided to try and interest a publisher in my red photos. A Study in Red. A way of looking at people and places from all over Europe through the colour red. There was interest shown. Two different publishers wanted to look at them.

Why am I telling you all this?

Because I want you to know that even though I had lost my baby over a year before I thought my life was back on track. I thought I was in control again. I had plans, a project, a new place to live. Rebirth.

When the cottage in Scotland was ready for me to move in I decided to drive up there in the camper van. It meant an overnight stop and I drove through North Yorkshire. I got to Little Madden about nine in the evening. I found a turn-off into the woods and parked. It wasn't allowed but I did it anyway. In the morning the woods were so beautiful that I decided to hang on for a few hours, look out for some bird life. Of course I lost track of the time. When I began to feel hungry I saw that it was past two o'clock. I walked out of the wood to the village and bought a drink and some chocolate. Then I walked back through the woods towards the place where I'd parked my van.

Don't forget I didn't know the area, so I ended up taking a few wrong paths. Then I saw a black car parked and walked towards it. Not far away, on the ground, was a baby. I was startled. It was the last thing I expected to find. I circled her and saw a young girl and a man lying on a blanket, fast asleep. I also saw the empty bottle of champagne. In a few seconds I summed the situation up. The baby had been left alone while the drunken couple cavorted and then slept it off. It angered me. My first instinct was to walk over and wake them up but I couldn't drag myself away from the baby. She was about the same size as Emily had been when I lost her. From somewhere deep inside me came this yearning, this hunger. It was like standing at the edge of a hole. A powerful urge came over me. The girl and the man had discarded this baby for their own pleasures. Anything could have come by: a fox, a dog, biting insects. Don't forget I knew about woodland. Underneath the trees and leaves and bushes was life teeming in many forms. Anything could have hurt the baby. I bent down. The baby was so solid, so rounded; her cheeks, shoulders, knees, her little hands in fists. I tried not to compare. My own baby was just a small, silent figure lying stiffly in the arms of the ambulance man. And here was this big, strong life, lying among the grass and leaves, placed at the edge of this couple's life, not in the middle, not in the heart of it as my baby had been.

I picked her up. I held her in my arms. She was hot and limp and she seemed to fit into the contours of my body. I hugged her and walked up and down for a moment, not really knowing what I was doing. It would serve them right, I thought, if they woke up and found the baby gone. Give them a shock if some right-minded person took the baby to the police station and said that it was being neglected.

Did I really intend that? I don't know. Those words certainly went through my head. Most likely I convinced myself that I was doing a good thing. Take the baby to a police station. Say that I'd found it asleep with its parents in a drunken stupor. Hand it over. Suggest that social services got involved. This line of thought ran through my head as I walked away, holding the baby tightly up to my chest.

My van was nearer than I'd thought. When I got there I put the baby on the bed in the back, made sure the pillow was there beside her so that she wouldn't roll off, and I drove away.

I didn't go to the police station. But you know that.

The baby slept for about an hour and I drove all of that time. What was I thinking? That I'd find a police station or pass a hospital and then I'd leave her somewhere? I can't remember exactly. I don't recall any firm ideas or words that went through my head, just some powerful need to have that baby with me.

I was driving on autopilot. When I did allow myself to consider the situation I imagined the little mite waking up at some point. She would cry for her mummy and then I'd take her back. She'd be upset so I'd absolutely have to do something.

She didn't cry. I stopped for petrol and bought some nappies and drink. Then I passed a sign for a campsite and I drove off the road. When I parked the camper she had woken up. I looked fearfully at her, waiting for her to scream, to alert passers-by, to let the world know that I was a stranger to her. But she just smiled at me. She was playing with her feet. I changed her nappy and held her up, close to me, talked to her. I got food out of the cool box, bananas and biscuits and milk, and she ate ravenously. We stayed there that night. And I waited for someone to knock on the door and ask me what I thought I was doing, taking a baby from its mother.

It was sometime the next day when I watched the news and heard the story that I realized that the couple had not been related to the baby. There was no mention of the man. The police were looking for a man in a black car who had abducted the baby. I was puzzled, confused. It was almost as if the reports were of a different baby that had been abducted, not the baby I had. I stayed in the campsite. I took the baby everywhere with me. I caught a bus and went into a nearby town and bought a pushchair. All the time I thought, someone will recognize the baby. They'll demand her return and I will be sent to prison. But nobody recognized her. Nobody thought it strange that I should buy a car seat or clothes or nappies or food. I was a woman with a baby. Nobody questioned it.

When I got to the cottage in Scotland the baby had been with me for five days. I had to call at the nearby house for the keys. The woman gave the baby an exaggerated smile the way that people do. The baby smiled back. The woman said, What a beautiful baby, what's her name? It's Emily, I said. How lovely! she replied.

I lived there for two years before buying a proper home for Emily and me. Every day, for a long time, I froze whenever the bell sounded or the telephone rang. I was always ready for them to come, to take Emily away. But no one did and in the end it was almost possible to believe that it had never happened.

In those first days I watched the news and I read the papers. There were suggestions of abuse. Did you know that? Jackie had been known to the social services. She had been charged with neglect of her older boys. I saw her making an appeal. She broke down. I felt my knees buckle. Her man put a big arm around her and then I noticed her huge stomach. Her baby was due soon, the newspapers said. When the reports came that she had given birth to a little girl I felt a weight fall off my shoulders. It was as if she had replaced her missing baby. I know that sounds ridiculous. No, it sounds callous, heartless, cruel, but I'm trying to be honest. She had other children, she had a new baby. I hoped in my heart that it would be easier for her because of that.

Emily has had a wonderful childhood. She has been loved, indulged and protected. She's a lovely, bright girl who is doing well at school. She plays the piano and loves to take photographs and is arty.

You'll wonder why I have approached you. Why I needed to tell you this story. I know that you had a bad time. The police didn't believe you. I know you moved away from your home town and your parents did as well. Most of all I know that you have lived for ten years not knowing what happened to little Lizzie. Possibly you thought her dead, maybe taken by a sick person, maybe murdered.

I wanted you to know that she is happy and well and has a better life than the one she would have had with her biological mother. What I did was wrong but it had a good outcome. I truly believe that.

What you do about this letter is up to you. I imagine you will consider passing it on to the police. What will happen then? They will take Emily away from me, the mother she loves, and place her back with Jackie Gilbert, a woman who didn't care much for her. Can you allow this to happen? I leave the decision to you. What happens to me is irrelevant.

I never told Emily that I was her biological mother. I told her that I had adopted her. In a way, that's exactly what happened.

Margaret Sloane

Terri tidied the pages up. She flicked through the photographs, hardly registering the small figure in each of them. She made a small pile and squared the corners. She looked up at the hotel. Her eye flicked from window to window.

She sat back. For ten years she thought Lizzie had been murdered.

She wriggled about in her seat. A boy came up to the table and took the glass that Margaret had been drinking from. He had a tower of glasses up against his chest. It looked precarious, as if it would topple if he added any more.

She picked up the papers and slid them back into the envelope. She stood up, her movements slow, uncertain. She put the envelope under her arm and realized then that she was still holding her car keys, had in fact been squeezing them so hard that her palm was red and sore. She put them into her bag and shook her hand, blowing cool air on it.

She walked across the hotel garden and went into the door where Margaret Sloane had gone. It took her into a long dark hallway and she clutched on to the envelope as she walked towards the front of the hotel and reception.

"Could you call Margaret Sloane, please? I'm not sure which room she is in."

"Margaret Sloane," the receptionist said brightly, "let me see."

The receptionist looked at a printed list that was in front of her. She held a ruler under a line of type and then moved it down the page, reading each line. She was shaking her head before she even got to the bottom.

"I'm sorry, we don't have anyone of that name staying here."

"Are you sure? A tall woman? She was wearing a dark mac? About forty five?"

"Actually we don't have any singles here at all. All our

guests are in double rooms, so I'm sorry, I can't help you."

A double room. Could it be that Margaret Sloane was here *with Lizzie*?

"Do you have a mother and daughter here?" she said, leaning closer to the counter, her voice a little louder.

"I'm sorry. I can't really give you any more information," the receptionist said, her smile gone, her expression wary.

"The daughter would be about twelve? Do you have a girl of about twelve staying here?" she said loudly, her hand pointing at the list of names.

A man appeared from the office behind. He was in a three-piece suit which was buttoned up. He had a book like a diary open in his hands.

"Can I help?" he said stiffly.

Terri turned away, half walked, half ran out of the front of the hotel and through the garden towards the car park. She slowed down as she got nearer, seeing, from a distance, that her car was sitting alone in a corner. The red car that had been next to it, Margaret Sloane's car, was gone.

She leaned against the driver's door and looked at the exit of the car park. She pictured the red car sitting there, maybe thirty minutes before, its indicator flashing on and off, then pulling out and sweeping away up the country lanes.

Maybe Margaret Sloane would have looked back for a moment. Maybe not.

TWENTY-SIX

Epping

The flat in Debden didn't seem so safe.

I paced up and down the small living room. I didn't know what to do. Mum was at the police station with Paula Bramble. I let my teeth knock together as I walked to the window and back to the door. I could hear the traffic from out in the street below, a car revving, the buzz of a motorbike, the wheeze of a lorry pulling its brakes on.

The blue bracelet. I tried to imagine it, lying in a toy box in the bedroom of Jade Henderson. It was wooden, hand painted. The flowers were bright yellow. Mum had loved it, wore it often. She had the matching earrings and she used to say, *I wish we'd bought the necklace as well!* Now the police had the bracelet and were questioning Mum about that night when Jade went missing. How had that bracelet gotten into Jade Henderson's bedroom? Mum had said that she'd never even been in the *house*.

There was an innocent explanation, I was sure. But what could it be?

I sat down on the armchair and realized that I didn't know what to do. Mum hadn't wanted me at the police station. Should I ring someone? Nana and Grandad? What would Mum say if I involved them? She would be annoyed. She hated it if her mum and dad interfered in her life. We only ever visited them once a year, sometime around Christmas, but it was always a duty. The person she was happiest with was *her* grandad, Paddy. Since he died and we moved to Epping, Mum hated to go back to her family at all.

Should I ring them? I stood up and looked for my mobile. I'd left it somewhere but wasn't sure where. I glanced across every surface in the room and then went into my bedroom. It was on the bed and I picked it up and noticed the corner of the brown envelope sticking out from under the duvet. My shoulders sagged and I sat down. Pictures of the girl, Lizzie Gilbert, growing up. Another mystery. Was there an innocent explanation for the brown envelope?

I fought back a growing feeling of dread. I had to keep focused, even though it seemed as though everything was falling away from me.

What was happening to my mum?

I thought back over the last weeks. The break up with Gerry, the application for a job in Liverpool, the increase in drinking. These things, in themselves, were not that unusual. When we lived in Whitby, Mum applied for a new job in London and we'd moved house. There'd been other men that she'd broken up with. She'd had periods of heavy drinking in the past but it had always tailed off and she'd gone back to being herself.

The story of the abducted baby and the photographs of the missing girl, these were extraordinary things. I hadn't even known about them until a few days before. Now there was a bracelet in Jade Henderson's bedroom. What was I to make of it all? There would be an explanation for it. I was sure there be *some way* of explaining it all.

I cradled my mobile. I couldn't ring Nana and Grandad, not until I'd spoken to Mum. I thought of ringing Robbie. I was sure if I told it all to him, he would know what to do. His mum, Sylvie, might come and pick me up, take me to their house, sit me in that long kitchen while she got busy phoning people, sorting it all out.

But I couldn't ring Robbie. That door had shut. I had to sort the situation out on my own.

I went into Mum's room and sat on her bed. I pulled the sheet up around me and stared at her open suitcase. It was messy, her clothes hanging over the edge, spilling out on to the floor. It was typical of Mum not to keep her stuff tidy. When she went to work she wore her suit and looked smart and organized. Her own room and her house was a different matter. It was why I did housework. I looked after her. Maybe that was one of my reasons for wanting to get a proper job – so that Mum would have to look after herself. A job in the city. How distant that possibility seemed now. Like a light in a remote window.

Would Mum become ill again? I wondered. Like she did when we were still living in Whitby?

I had been at primary school and Mum couldn't go to work. *What's up, princess?* Grandad Paddy had said. He spent a lot of time at our house, getting me up in the morning and off to school. He said that Mum was *poorly*.

She went to the doctor's, I knew, but she didn't seem to be ill in the sense that I, as a child, understood it. She looked the same and wasn't coughing or being sick or sitting on the toilet for hours. She wasn't in any pain and she didn't have any spots or rashes.

She stayed in her room a lot. Sometimes she didn't get dressed, didn't even get out of bed. She liked me to lie beside her and sometimes she hugged me so tightly that I couldn't move and we'd have a bit of a play fight where I would break free. But it only lasted a few seconds because she didn't seem to have the strength to play properly.

She cried a lot. I didn't actually *see* her crying but her face was often red and she sniffed loudly and there were little screwed-up white tissues everywhere. Now and again I would find her sitting in the kitchen staring out of the window. She'd say hello to me and her voice would crack and then the sniffing and the nose-blowing would start. *Silly me!* she'd say. *This hay fever!* I was only young but I knew what crying was. I spent lots of time sitting in the kitchen while Grandad Paddy cooked for me. He would pause as he was frying an egg or making some toast and listen at the door. At first I thought he was waiting for Mum to shout out a food order but I realized that he was making sure that she wasn't lying in her bedroom sobbing. *Mum's all right!* he would say, winking at me, fluffing up my hair. When Nana and Grandad arrived, Grandad Paddy said rudely, *What do you two want?* Nana looked after me for a while and Grandad Paddy stayed at his own house. Eventually Mum appeared more and more. I saw her cooking some spaghetti, ironing some clothes, putting some mascara on in the hall mirror. Nana and Grandad went home and then Grandad Paddy appeared at the door. *How are my princesses?* he said.

I got out of Mum's bed. I squatted down at her case and started to tidy it. I needed to *do* something. Get hold of someone who could help us, who would know what to do. A name came into my head. I sorted through Mum's clothes until I came to the jacket she'd been wearing on the day we'd left our house and come to the flat. From the top pocket I pulled out a small card with a bathtub printed on it. I read the phone number and dialled it on my mobile. A few seconds later a male voice answered.

"Is that Raymond?" I said.

"Yep," he said.

"The plumber?" I said, for no good reason.

"Yeah. I don't do emergency call-outs, though. I can give you a number of someone who does. . ."

"No, Raymond, it's Stella Parfitt. Your neighbour? I don't know what to do. The police have arrested my mum. I didn't know who to call only you've helped us out in the past and Mum likes you. . ."

I told him about the bracelet. I was stuttering and repeating myself, my words gushing out. He let me go on for a few minutes and then calmly asked for the address of the flat. I gave it to him. When he ended the call I stood up and looked round the tiny room and felt completely hemmed in. I gave Mum's case a half-hearted kick. How had we ended up like this? In a poky flat, living out of suitcases, my poor mum facing questions in a police interview room.

Why were we there? For our own protection?

I didn't feel protected. I felt adrift, as if me and Mum had stepped off our own boat on to some flimsy raft and were floating away. Now Mum was gone and I was sitting on my own not knowing what to do.

I made a decision.

I packed Mum's clothes in her case. I walked around the other rooms collecting anything that belonged to me or Mum. Then I went into my room and packed my case. I carried the cases out and lined them up by the door and went into the kitchen. I washed the dishes and put them away and emptied the contents of the fridge into a bin bag, pouring away the unused milk down the sink. I took the bin bag out and put it into a plastic bin along the landing. Then I closed the front door and carried the suitcases down the stairs.

I stood in front of the flats and waited. It was almost dark, the air pleasantly warm on my skin, the street busy with young people hanging around in groups. A couple were out on their own, their arms around each other in a deep kiss, oblivious of the fact that they were in full view of everyone. I wondered if Jack Slater was prowling around, looking for someone's ear to blow into.

The van pulled up across the road, the bathtub standing out under the street lights. Raymond got out and walked towards me, pulling his T-shirt down over his belly.

"All right, kid?" he said, looking at me and then at the suitcases.

"I'm going home," I said. "Will you take me there and then down to the police station to see what's happened to Mum?"

"No problem," he said.

I didn't look back as we drove away from the safe flat.

TWENTY-SEVEN

Raymond asked me about the police. I explained what had happened, what Paula Bramble had said, as clearly as I could.

"This is daft," he said. "There'll be some reason that the bracelet was there. Maybe your mum dropped it when she was walking along and one of the Hendersons picked it up. You know those kiddies are always hanging around the street."

His reaction made me feel instantly better. It was ridiculous that the police were even considering Mum. Raymond could see it, I could see it. Anyone who knew Mum would be able to see it. The rest of the stuff, the photographs, were something else entirely. An insistent beep at the back of my head that would have to be answered later.

The journey didn't take long. Soon we were on the high street heading for Forest Lane. I looked gratefully at Raymond. I'd been rude about him in the past. He was always helping us out with one thing and another. When we were burgled it had taken him a whole day to mend our back door and put a lock on the garden gate. Mum said that he hadn't taken a penny for it, just the cost of the lock. And he had saved us from the mob who had been waiting for Mum.

"How's Samantha?" I said.

Samantha, his daughter, lived with his ex-wife.

"She's great," Ray said. "She's nagging me for a mobile phone!"

"She's not that old, surely," I said.

"Ten," he said. "I said I'd buy her one when she goes to big school."

I thought of my own mobile. As we turned into Forest Lane I felt my pockets and remembered calling Raymond on it. I'd packed it, I was sure. I was picturing it lying in the suitcase as we drove past the Hendersons'. I caught a glimpse of the bungalow. It was completely dark, in contrast to the adjoining one next door, which had all its lights on. It looked eerie, or maybe I thought that because I knew what had happened there. I wondered where the Hendersons were. In a *safe* house somewhere? The sound of the handbrake creaking interrupted my train of thought and I realized that we had stopped and were sitting outside my house. In front of us, a few metres up the lane, was the cable van, its colours muted by the darkness. I got out and waited while Ray got the cases from the back. I avoided looking at our front window, still covered with planks.

"Your mum'll be all right," Raymond said, carrying the cases to the front door and putting them down on the step. "Give me a few minutes to get changed and we'll go down the station and see what's happening."

"OK."

Would Mum be all right? I thought of her illness. In my mind she'd lain in bed for weeks but possibly I'd exaggerated that. Maybe it had only been days. Grandad Paddy had fussed round her, nothing had been too much trouble for one of his princesses. What was happening to her now? In the police station? Nobody would be fussing around her there.

I got my keys out and went into the house. I clicked the hall light on and saw letters and leaflets scattered across the hall rug. It reminded me of returning home after a holiday. Some holiday. I put the cases on the floor and picked up the letters. There was one for me. I held on to it while I walked gingerly around, leaning into rooms and putting the lights on as if I half expected a crowd of neighbours to be lying in wait for me. Each room looked exactly the same as when we'd left it, the TV remotes lying at angles on the settee, the glasses upended on the drainer, the newspaper open on the kitchen table. Mum had been reading it when the journalists made their way to her front door.

I went upstairs and did the same thing, checking each room, leaving the lights on so that the house was bright and welcoming, not dark and empty like the Hendersons' place had been.

I went into Mum's bedroom and turned the computer on. I looked out of the window at the forest while the computer loaded, making mechanical grunting noises as it did so. All I could see were dark swathes, the mass of the forest darker than the night sky, looking thick and

196

impenetrable. Somebody had taken Jade Henderson into that forest. Would she ever come out? I wondered.

I opened my letter. It was from one of the agencies I had visited. It was an interview for a job in an Australian bank. I put it down on the desk. The computer had loaded and I sat down for a minute and clicked on the email. I scrolled down sixty-two messages, most of them to do with Mum's work. In the middle was one from my friend Grace. I opened it. *Sorry about all the probs. Come round my place. Sleep over. We can catch up on gossip. Susie says to tell you that we're boycotting the newspapers. Not that we read them much anyway. Love and kisses. Grace.*

I reread it and felt this flood of emotion. It was only a few words but it felt like someone was reaching out to me, trying to pull me out of whatever deep water I'd fallen into. I pressed the print button. I wanted a copy of it.

While it printed I looked again at the letter about the job interview. Hadn't it all started like this days before? Me picking up a letter on Mum's desk for a job interview in Liverpool? At the time I had been miffed because Mum hadn't told me about it. How ironic that now seemed. The truth was I had known almost nothing of the really important bits of Mum's life.

The front doorbell sounded for just a second. A trill ring and then quiet, as if someone was trying not to make too much noise. It would be Raymond. I went downstairs. I opened the front door and he was standing there in a suit, white shirt and tie. He looked as though he were going to see his bank manager again.

"People always treat me better if I'm dressed like this," he explained.

"Let's go, then," I said.

The distant sound of my mobile made me stop. It was coming from my suitcase there in the hall. I bent down and opened it, sticking my hand in and searching for it. I pulled it out and looked at the screen. The word *Mum* was there. I answered it.

"Stel, they've let me go."

"What's happened?"

"I'll explain when I see you. I'm still at the station but Paula's going to give me a lift to the flat."

"I'm not at the flat. I'm at home. I packed our bags. Raymond gave me a lift."

"Oh, that's good. That's such good news. I'll be there soon and I'll explain when I see you."

The call ended.

"They're letting her go," I said, amazed. "She's coming home!"

"That's great. I'll be off then."

"No, you stay. Mum'll want to thank you. You should stay, honestly."

He thought about it for a moment.

"I'll get changed," he said, "then I'll be back."

The door closed behind him and I went into the kitchen, sat down at the table and waited.

TWENTY-EIGHT

Mum looked flushed when she came in, her eyes shining. It was the happiest I'd seen her for days. Raymond, wearing a clean shirt and jeans, gave her a little hug and said how pleased he was to see her. *What's happened?* I kept saying, wanting to know why they'd let her go. Paula Bramble looked happy but her smile wasn't as bright as Mum's.

"I'll go now, Terri. You should be with Stella. You shouldn't get any more trouble from. . ." she made a gesture with her hands, "from anyone. If you do, you have my number."

My mum nodded. Then she gave Paula a hug. I was surprised. Hadn't she been biting the policewoman's head off for days? Calling her *Inspector*? Paula patted my mum on her back and then went, my mum following her out to the front door. I heard it close, then Mum returned.

"Well?" I said.

"You know the burglary we had?" she said, looking from me to Raymond and back again.

"The laptop went and my bag was stolen. In it was my money, my credit card and my mobile. It was Vince Henderson who broke into the house. They found my credit card in his room."

Vince Henderson. Always on his own at school, always with a sneer on his face.

"The police continued their fingertip search. That was the reason they found my blue bracelet in the first place. Well, under the boy's carpet were a whole load of credit cards, not just mine. They didn't find my bag or anything, he must have got rid of that."

"The bracelet was in your bag!" I said, the penny finally dropping.

"I must have taken it off and put it in there. Then he broke in here, took my bag and for some reason kept the bracelet."

"Maybe the baby found the bracelet. You know how inquisitive small children are," Raymond said.

We went quiet. Maybe each of us was imagining Jade Henderson finding the blue bracelet, playing with it, toddling back to her room with it. It made me feel stricken for a moment. Amid the delight of my mum's return I felt this tightness in my stomach. Jade Henderson was like the unwelcome guest at this happy reunion.

"My Samantha loves jewellery," Ray said quietly, as if talking to himself.

"Have the police arrested Vince?" I said.

Mum shook her head.

"It's not a priority. Could you imagine them arresting him while his sister's still missing? Imagine his mum and dad. They'll deal with it later. It's not like I'm going to push them into doing it."

"Still no news on the little girl?" Raymond said.

"Nothing. Paula said that they're still searching the forest. It's such a big area."

"Six thousand acres," Raymond said. "It stretches for twelve miles."

Mum didn't answer. She had picked up a bottle of wine and was reaching for the corkscrew. I wondered how big the wood at Little Madden was. Nowhere near as big as Epping. Mum pulled the cork out of the bottle easily. She looked at me and Raymond.

"I don't want any," I said.

"Me neither, Terri. I'm going to leave you two alone. I'll pop round in the morning and measure up the glass for the front window. That's if you want me to."

"I do, I do," Mum said, pulling a stemmed glass from the cupboard and filling it. "I'm so grateful for all your help."

"See you in the morning, then," Raymond said, giving a sheepish smile.

Mum followed him up the hall and I heard them talking, both their voices low. I looked over at the wine and thought about the things that Mum and I had to talk about. I heard the front door shut and picked up her glass. I walked out into the hall and handed it to her.

"You'll need this," I said. "There's some stuff we have to talk about."

"What?" she said, a flash of concern crossing her face.

"I found the photographs of Lizzie Gilbert. I want to know about them."

She looked at me and took a gulp of her wine.

"I want the truth this time, Mum. I want you to tell me everything."

"You'd better bring the whole bottle, then. It's a long story," she said.

TWENTY-NINE

Whitby

The police station in Whitby was on a hill. It was a couple of roads back from the harbour, so the smell of the sea was strong and the sound of the gulls circling above was piercingly loud. It was set away from the shops and the crowds that bustled through the streets on summer days. It was much bigger than the police house in Little Madden but it still had rigid opening and closing times. Eight in the morning until eight in the evening. Twelve hours to catch criminals. At other times there was an emergency phone number.

Not that Terri was there for an *emergency*.

She had walked from home. It took fifteen minutes. She stood across the road from it. A two-storey building that had a noticeboard outside. She made a step as if to cross the road and go towards the entrance but something stopped her. She clutched at her bag, her fingers finding the opening and pushing down inside until she felt the roughness of the envelope, its corners, its opening. She imagined standing at the counter and laying it down, a pile of pages and photographs. A policeman would look up from what he was doing, glance at the paper and then slowly turn his eyes on to her.

Her chest felt tight and she began to breathe quickly, too quickly. She looked around and saw, a few metres along, a bus shelter. She went towards it, her hands on her ribs, counting the breaths in and out. She leant against the frame and gazed through the traffic at the squat building across the road.

Terri knew Whitby police station from when she first stayed with her grandad. She had made a number of visits there during the aftermath of Lizzie's disappearance. Mostly the police took her back to Little Madden, back to the wood, back to the town, going over and over her story. Weeks later, though, when they'd covered all the ground, when they'd dragged her here and there, when they'd found out nothing, they set up prearranged times and asked her to report to the Whitby station, where she was met by Inspector Williams and interviewed all over again. The local police eyed her suspiciously when she was sitting in the reception waiting for her appointment.

When the meetings stopped she had no reason to go there again.

Now, ten years later, she had good reason. In her bag was the letter and photographs that Margaret Sloane had given her a week before. The explanation of what had happened to Lizzie. It would be called evidence, she supposed. Certainly it would prove, beyond a doubt, that she had had nothing to do with Lizzie's disappearance.

A bus pulled up and some people got off. It moved away again and she stared at the station for what seemed like a long time.

Returning to Whitby after her meeting with Margaret Sloane, she had lived in a kind of shocked state. For days she had been seething, on the edge of shouting at everyone. She'd read the letter and reread it, focusing on every detail of Margaret's story. Why hadn't she walked out of her house one day and gone straight to the police? That would have been the most sensible thing to do. But Terri had felt paralysed by what she had read. She'd hidden the envelope in various places in her bedroom: a drawer, underneath her bed, at the bottom of her wardrobe. She'd tried to get on with other things: ironing, dusting, looking at her bills, tidying up her work bag. Each time, though, she felt her shoulders turning towards it, her eyes pulled back to the envelope.

The photographs stung her. There were pictures of Lizzie at different ages, the most recent showing her as skinny, wearing shorts and a tight top, her hair up in a funny high ponytail. On the cusp of being a teenager – wearing grown-up clothes but still with the body of a child, her shape angular, her chest flat. A much younger one showed Lizzie in a paddling pool, the day bright so that picture looked as though it was flooded with white light. Lizzie had a sun hat on and was holding a bucket out to someone, maybe the person taking the photo. Margaret Sloane, the woman who had stolen her. The ghost behind the camera.

Putting down the photographs, she found herself looking at the letter again, the edges of it crinkled and floppy where she'd held it over and over. Even though the events had been painstakingly described she had wanted to know more. She had wanted to interrogate Margaret. Everyone had interrogated her in those months after the disappearance. Wasn't it Margaret's turn?

Had Margaret passed anyone while walking out of Little Madden Wood towards her camper van? There had been people around, Terri had seen them when she had run down to the lake or when she was pushing the empty pushchair here and there. And where was the campsite? Terri had visited campsites in North Yorkshire when she was younger, on trips with the church. Had it been one that she had stayed at? Had the camper van been parked across the way from the place that they had pitched their tents all those years before? She wanted to know. It was important to her to visualize the whole story from beginning to end.

Why hadn't Terri gone straight to the police? In Little Madden? In Printon? Why hadn't she taken Margaret's letter and the photographs and given them to the self-same policeman, Inspector Williams, who had questioned her for days and days, calling her a liar, telling her to own up. *Tell us what happened to Lizzie,* he had said. *Did she fall over and bang her head? Did she choke on her own vomit? Did you panic, hide her under leaves or bushes? Did you bury her? Tell us. We'll understand. We'll be able to forgive you. It's only by being honest that you can forgive yourself.*

Terri put a hand in front of her face, trying to block out the memory from ten years before. Then, moments later, she dropped it and saw that she had been joined by a girl and boy who had turned up in the bus shelter. The boy had his arm around the girl's neck as though he was in a kind of rugby tackle. From time to time he leant down and kissed her, short and sloppily.

She could hear a plane circling above, its noise like a moving drill.

She hadn't gone to the police because she didn't want them to know about her and Steve Ryan. About them lying on a blanket, the empty champagne bottle beside them, asleep when they should have been looking after Lizzie. That was the bald truth.

They would also know about the black car.

She hadn't wanted to lie. She had never intended to say anything about a man in a black car but the words had just come out and then taken a life of their own until it seemed possible that *something like that had actually happened*. Instead it had been a woman who took Lizzie. Nobody had stopped her or questioned her. Not even when she was buying baby goods. No one had glanced at the baby or the woman as they ran away to a remote cottage in Scotland.

Another bus came and she moved out of the way as a mum with a small boy got off the platform carrying bags of shopping and pulling behind her a folded-up pushchair. The boy and girl further along stopped their kissing. Amid a series of grunts they took the shopping from the woman and assembled the pushchair, and then all of them walked off up the road.

Those reasons weren't enough to stop her going to the

police. She had lied, she had covered up the truth. But the heart of the story, the missing baby, had happened. She'd been young, eighteen years old, she'd been traumatized. She hadn't known what she was doing. Now she was a mother. She knew what was right and what was wrong. It had taken her seven days to come to this conclusion but she knew what to do. She'd thought of Stella. The idea of her daughter being taken made Terri feel faint, as if there wasn't enough air for her to breathe, as if she was in a tiny space and couldn't get out.

She walked out of the bus shelter and waited a few moments before crossing the road. The cars were queuing along one side and she walked between a couple peering out on the other side in case a motorcyclist came along. Then she continued. Outside the police station she stood for a moment. She *was* doing the right thing.

She put her hand in her bag and felt for one of the photographs. She pulled it out and stood in the middle of the pavement looking at it. It was one of Lizzie in a school uniform, a dark blazer and skirt. In front of her she was holding something. It was too small to see what it was but Terri had a pretty good idea what it might have been. A certificate. Maybe for swimming or music or good work or charity fund-raising. Stella had three from her school and they had put them into little frames on the wall. Lizzie must have had done something really outstanding and been rewarded for it.

Margaret had said that Lizzie had had a *wonderful childhood*. She had been *loved, indulged, protected*, Margaret said. Just like her Stella. Poor Lizzie certainly hadn't had much of that when she lived with Jackie Gilbert. A picture came into her head then, something that she hadn't thought of for many years. An upstairs room in Jackie Gilbert's house. The lock on the outside of the children's bedroom door. It had been clumsily fixed on, she remembered. Kirk had done it, she thought. Not a strong bolt. It could have been broken by an adult pushing hard against the door but not by a small child locked in. Not by Lizzie or either of the boys. It had given her a lump in her throat at the time. Afterwards, when Lizzie had been taken, she'd forgotten all about it.

Margaret was almost certainly right when she said that Lizzie had had a better life with her than the one she should have had with her mother. *I love her more than anything*, Margaret had said. Had Jackie loved Lizzie more than anything? Had Jackie loved Lizzie at all?

Terri put the photo back in her bag and walked on past the police station up to a corner. She stopped. Going to the police, showing them Margaret's letter was the right thing to do. But was it the right thing to do for Lizzie now? She thought Margaret was her mother. The police would knock on her door and take her away, perhaps back to Jackie Gilbert or failing that, into some kind of foster care. Lizzie, who had been stolen from her mother once, would endure the same fate again, stolen from the only mother she had ever known.

Could Terri do that?

She shook her head fiercely. A woman passed her and

looked enquiringly at her. People would think she was mad if she stood out in the middle of the street talking to herself. She patted her bag and walked back across the road. She wanted to see Stella. She needed to hold her little girl, to give her a bear hug, to feel her ribs and her bony arms, to smell her strawberry hair shampoo, to stroke her taut hot skin, to run her fingers through her tangled-up hair, to hear her stories about dragons or vampire bats. She was only fifteen minutes from home and she walked at first but then increased her speed and was virtually running by the time she got to Grandad's door. He opened it with a puzzled expression.

"I thought you were out for a few hours?"

She rushed past him into the kitchen, where Stella was getting some ice and lemon for the jug of water they would have with their lunch.

"Mum?" Stella said, looking worried.

Terri didn't answer. She stepped across and threw her arms around her daughter. She held her like that for as long as Stella would allow it. Then she stepped back and stood awkwardly against the wall.

"What's up?" Grandad said.

"I need a drink," Terri said.

Stella held up the jug.

"No, a much stronger drink than that," she said.

THIRTY

Terri's illness lasted for weeks. The doctor said she was suffering from depression. She stayed in bed, in her room. Sometimes Stella was there with her but mostly she was on her own. Grandad took over the running of her life. She saw his worried face at her door and heard him clattering around in the kitchen. When she got up and started to go out it was small trips, a few breaths of fresh air along the street and then back into the flat. As the days went by she became stronger and went further afield, sometimes with Grandad, mostly on her own.

She walked around Whitby, vanishing among the summer crowds, like a tourist. Occasionally she went across the harbour bridge and into the old part of the town, up the small winding streets that led to the abbey. She paused at seaside gift shops and tea rooms and ice-cream parlours. She often stopped at the window of a shop that sold Whitby Jet, polished black stones that had once been lumps of fossilized driftwood dug up from the beaches. Now it was jewellery. She liked looking at it. The colour suited her mood. It hung from earrings and on chains, like black tears.

A few doors along was a tattoo parlour, *Veronica: Tattoo Artist*. She often paused outside it. It had no window, just boards on which there were examples of the designs. She looked at the dragons and bulls, the snakes and birds. There were people's names: Mum, Sally, Mary, Manchester United. There were flowers too, roses mainly but in the corner she saw an unusual one: a single blue flower, like a buttonhole. She wasn't sure what it was. Then she remembered. A forget-me-not.

Sometimes she looked at the letter and the photographs. She'd done the right thing for Lizzie. She knew she had. That's why she folded the letter over and over and stuck it firmly in the bottom of the envelope and then tucked the envelope in the bottom of her wardrobe.

She made herself do more and more. She shopped, picked up Stella from school. Eventually she rang up work and made arrangements to go back. One Monday in August she got up early, pulled out her suit and shirt, things she hadn't worn for weeks. Then she glanced down and saw the envelope pushed into a small space between her shoes and boots. It stuck out untidily and the sight of it made her stomach lurch.

She forced herself out, along the streets, dressed for work but not heading there. She quickened her step towards the harbour bridge and then crossed the water, the gulls circling in wheels above her, cackling and screeching together, swooping down in ones and twos on the fishing boats that went underneath.

She got to the tattoo parlour. It was closed. She was too early. She decided to wait and paced up and down the street until a small dark lady in a white overall and clogs got out of a taxi. She pulled a giant bunch of keys from a bag and opened the door.

"What can I do for you?" she said, clicking the lights on inside the windowless interior.

She was older than Terri first thought, her dark hair dyed, deep lines round her eyes and mouth.

"Are you Veronica?"

"I am." She smiled, walking across to a couch and clicking on a nearby fan.

"I want a tattoo," Terri said. "The blue flower on the board outside. The forget-me-not."

"*Vergissmeinnicht*," Veronica said, flicking through a ring binder until she came to a picture of the flower.

Terri frowned.

"That's the German word for it. I always think it sounds nicer."

"Can you do it now?" Terri said.

"Afraid you might change your mind, young lady? Wouldn't it be better to think it over?"

"No, I'd like it done now," she said, taking her suit jacket off and unbuttoning her shirt.

"If you say so, dear," Veronica said, pulling out a tray of inks and pens.

There was music playing while Veronica got ready, washing her hands, rubbing the soap in between her fingers like a surgeon. It was jazzy, old-fashioned, with a lot of saxophone. After telling Terri that it would hurt Veronica was silent, concentrating on the job she was doing. Terri lay back and felt the insertions like tiny burns on her skin. She looked round from time to time and saw small beads of blood appear which were wiped clear by Veronica. She closed her eyes and let the music fill her head. All the while the German word *Vergissmeinnicht* repeated itself over and over in her mind. Veronica was right. Forget-me-not sounded childlike. *Vergissmeinnicht* was fluid and sibilant. It suggested regret and sorrow and longing.

All of the things that Terri felt.

Later that night she lit a fire in the garden. Stella's friend Sadie had come round and they were making a den in her bedroom. She could hear the shrieks and giggles and whispers as she passed the door.

Terri's arms were bare. The tattoo felt swollen, bruised, sore. She wasn't to touch it. She was to wait for the flower to emerge from the scabbed skin. She wondered what Grandad would say. Stella had been concerned, thinking Terri had had an accident. *Does it hurt very much, Mum?* she had said but Terri shook her head and mussed up Stella's hair.

The fire had taken hold and the wood was burning, making cracking sounds. She opened the envelope and took out the letter and photographs. She glanced back at the windows of the flat to make sure that Stella wasn't looking. Then she fed the pages one by one into the flames, waiting for each to blacken and fold before putting the next one in.

When it was done she stood back from the heat and felt a cooling breeze lift her hair and brush against her sore skin.

It was over.

THIRTY-ONE

Epping

Mum talked until late, past two o'clock. She was on her bed and I sat on the chair. I listened while she explained. Sometimes she sat up, sometimes she lay back. Occasionally she swivelled round, lifted her feet on to the ground and looked as though she was about to stand up. She drank her wine slowly, filling her glass up before it was quite empty.

I listened to the whole story with growing dismay. Some of it she told flatly, with little emotion. Now and then her voice cracked and she looked like she was on the brink of tears. She was defensive at times, as if I was openly disagreeing with her. *I did what I thought was best at the time!* she said over and over. She kept going till she was too tired to carry on. Towards the end she kept repeating the same sentence, *Lizzie has had a better life than she would have had with her own mother.* The red wine finally forced her to close her eyes just before two. I covered her up with a sheet and went next door to my own room, where I lay awake for a long time.

I was feeling a lot of emotions at once. I'd listened to her a week before when she first told me about the baby. I'd been upset then because she kept me in the dark. Now that she'd told me the complete truth I felt angry. She'd lied to me. She'd lied to everyone.

For over twenty years she had kept this secret inside her, just a few hastily uttered words she had told and never been able to take back. A man in a black car. I had believed her. End of story. I'd imagined it, a car sliding silently through the trees, a nondescript man stepping out of the driver's door. I had pictured him dressed from head to toe in black, like a secret agent. A villain. With one hand he had pushed Mum over and with the other he'd snatched the baby. But it was just a fiction to cover up what had really happened.

There were only four people who knew about it: Mum, the married man, me and the woman who called herself Margaret.

I could not sleep. I got out of bed and went downstairs. It felt strange being back in my own house after spending five days in the tiny flat. Everywhere felt bigger and certain things looked unfamiliar. The hallway seemed huge, the ceiling higher than before, the parquet floor darker, as if it had been varnished when we were away. The living room was odder. The boards over the broken window made it seem like a film set in some war drama. On the floor was the broken glass; some of the pieces were large enough to be picked up with care; others were tiny lethal shards. It would all have to be swept up and taken to the rubbish dump.

If only everything else could be cleared up so easily.

I wandered through the kitchen without turning the

lights on. I opened the back door and stood looking out into the garden. I thought about the married man. I was full of rage towards him. He had known the truth and he had kept quiet to protect his own character, his own family. If he had come forward, if he had taken his share of the blame, then Mum wouldn't have had to go through her whole adult life keeping this horrible secret, having everyone blame her and suspect her of hurting the baby. I tried to visualize him. I pictured some of the men Mum had been with over the years. It didn't help. He'd probably been nice looking, a bit vain, worried about his clothes. Maybe he'd been married too young. I'd seen well-dressed men like that. They drove racy cars with child seats in the back. I'd watched them idling at the traffic lights, looking longingly out at the schoolgirls passing by.

Then there was the woman who called herself Margaret. I felt furious with her. Why hadn't she just left Mum alone?

In the ten years since she disappeared she had sent the photos to Mum's work. Every year, on the date that the baby was taken, a photo had arrived showing the girl growing from a teenager to a young woman. Why hadn't she just left it? Why torture Mum every year with a reminder of the whole sorry story?

I walked out into the garden. The air felt chilly and I hugged myself. There was an almost-full moon and it lit up the garden, giving it a silver hue. The trees and bushes seemed to stand taller, their foliage stretched out. The grass seemed crisper underfoot. How different it was to the night that Jade Henderson had been taken. Then the air had been spongy, the heat clinging to everything, the night sky busy with clouds racing here and there, the promise of rain like a whisper through the forest.

Margaret had wanted Mum to know so that she wouldn't think that the baby had been murdered. Why couldn't she have just left things the way they were? Mum had only had one secret then, a lie that she had told. After Margaret went she had a whole story to conceal.

Why hadn't she gone to the police? I would have. As soon I saw the woman with her photographs and her confessions I'd have gone to the police. Wasn't that what any sensible person would have done? But Mum wasn't always rational. She did things from the heart. Like the men she chose. They were unsuitable, too young, too self centred. She made bad decisions.

Her worst decision had been to keep Margaret's secret.

I sat on a garden chair and stared at the sky. It was a deep inky blue, the moon shiny like satin. At the far corner of the sky the blue was lighter, hinting at daylight. I stretched my arms up and felt my joints crack.

Tomorrow I would talk to Mum properly. Tell her she should stop faffing about and go to the police. Maybe tell it all to Paula Bramble. Hadn't they hugged a couple of hours before? It was time to unload everything. To expose Margaret and the married man. Both of them had got off scot-free and my mum had lived under the weight of it. So what if the young woman found out about her past? She'd be twenty-one, old enough to make her own decisions.

And Mum wouldn't have to carry it all round with her.

I thought of Jackie Gilbert. What would it be like for her to find it all out after so many years? An uncomfortable feeling took hold of me. I stood up, turning my back on the garden. I went inside and locked the back door, taking the key out and leaving it on the side. I turned the lights off and went upstairs. Jackie Gilbert had a right to know. Wouldn't it *at least* make her feel better to know that her daughter hadn't been murdered?

I could hear Mum snoring lightly from the next room. She was in a deep sleep but I was wide awake sitting on the side of my bed. I thought of the week before, when the house was besieged with journalists and Mrs Henderson had come walking up the street, her clothes flying out at each side of her, her finger on our doorbell, her cries, *What have you done with my baby!* It made me feel light-headed all of a sudden. Her big frame, her pregnant belly, her flowing dresses, all these things made her a figure of fun. But on that night she came along the street like a tigress, feral in her need to find out what had happened to her daughter.

Would Jackie Gilbert be like that?

I lay down. Tomorrow I would tell Mum what I thought she should do.

Mum took it badly.

"Don't be ridiculous! After all this time? I'm not going to the police now! What good would it do?"

She was sitting at the kitchen table cradling a glass of

water that she had filled and refilled from the tap. She looked awful. Her lips were dry and she had bags under her eyes. She was wearing an old T-shirt with a rip at the shoulder and some cut-off jeans.

I'd opened the back door and the sun was shining in. It seemed like a good day. We were back at home. The neighbours would soon know that Mum had nothing to do with the disappearance of Jade. Lots of the problems of the last week would be over and we could go back to normal. Except that there was this *thing* hanging between us. This uncomfortable story that Mum had chosen to keep inside her.

It had to come out. For everyone's sake.

"For Jackie Gilbert? Doesn't she deserve to know what happened to her daughter?" I said gently.

"What good would it do? She won't be able to find her! How would that make her feel? She's had twenty years of coming to terms with the death of her daughter and now I'm going to tell her that it was all a lie and her daughter is alive and well but – hey! Sorry! – I don't know where. How will that do Jackie any good?"

"But it's the *truth*. The truth is always better than a lie."

"Is it? You're young. Everything's black and white to you. You don't understand!"

This annoyed me. I was old enough when Mum wanted it. I looked after her and looked after the house. When she couldn't argue her way out of things it was because I was too young. Just like when we were talking about her poor choice of boyfriends.

"What about Lizzie, the young woman? She will never know her own mother and – didn't you say she had brothers? What about them? She has a whole family she doesn't know about."

"Even if I told it all now they'd never be able to find her," Mum said fiercely.

"You have the photos that Margaret sent year by year. There may be clues there."

"You can't even tell whether it's England or abroad! It could be Australia? New Zealand? How could they find them there? That's the point, Stel. Even if I told every bit of the truth, who would it help? Jackie still wouldn't have her daughter back."

"But she'd know that her baby hadn't been murdered."

She was quiet for a moment. She took a big mouthful of water and licked her lips.

"If by some amazing piece of detective work the police found Lizzie Gilbert and someone said to her, *Here's your real mum!*, what would she say or think? She'd have no memories of her birth mother. Which is just as well because Jackie didn't particularly care for her when she was a baby."

"You're judging her. If she'd been a better mother, would you have told the truth?"

"No. Yes . . . I don't know."

"You're playing at being God."

"I don't believe in God."

"But you're still making decisions for someone else."

She was quiet and I began to feel a little hopeful. Was

she coming round to my point of view? Couldn't she see that if she unburdened herself then it would be someone else's problem?

"Sit down, Stella."

I pursed my lips. Calling me *Stella* was not a good sign.

"Throughout all of this I tried to do the best I could at the time. I screwed up. I know I did, but in the end my decision not to tell the police was based on one important thing. I felt responsible for Lizzie being abducted in the first place."

I went to speak but she put her hand up to stop me.

"If I hadn't been messing around, drinking. If I hadn't been infatuated with that man. Nothing would have happened to her. So, ten years later when I had to make a decision I made it for Lizzie. Not for Jackie or Margaret or not even for me. I had to think what would be best for her. After ten years away from her mother, living with a woman who adored her, who was giving her the kind of life that Jackie wouldn't have given her. . ."

"You can't say that!"

"I can say that. I saw it with my own eyes. Jackie didn't care a jot for Lizzie."

"But if she got her back, she might have learned her lesson."

"OK, just supposing, somehow, I had found where Margaret was living. What if I exposed Margaret and what she had done all those years before, what would that have done to Lizzie? Taken away the only home she had ever known? Put her adoptive mother in prison? Introduced her to a family she didn't know? What was the point of any of that? I decided to leave things as they were. That's why I burned it all. That's why I closed it up in some little box in my head. I can live with it. I *have* lived with it."

"I don't know if I can live with it," I said.

"That's up to you, Stella. I've tried to be honest, finally, with you. I don't want you to go to the police but if you do I won't blame you."

She stood up just as there was a ring on the front door. I went out to open it, my heart heavy, my mood low. My mum was flaky about a lot of things but sometimes she was immovable, her soft, girly front hiding a rock-hard centre.

I opened the door and Paula Bramble was there. Her hair was flat, hooked behind her ears. She was wearing the same clothes she'd had on the previous evening. She'd been working all night.

"Just checking that you're all right," Paula said tentatively, as though she thought one of us might bite her head off.

I held the door open. I followed her as she walked into the kitchen. My mum looked up expectantly.

"I've got some news, actually. There's been some developments. We're talking to someone who we hope will give us a firm lead on the whereabouts of Jade. I can't say any more than that."

"You sound like a press release," Mum said sourly.

"Sorry, Terri. It's police-speak. You know I can't tell you any more. The main thing for you is that you are definitely off the hook."

"Surely the *main thing* is to find Jade," Mum said.

I stared at Mum. Why was she being so horrible to Paula? None of it was her fault.

"I'll go," Paula said, "I've obviously come at a bad time."

"Mum, wasn't there something you wanted to say to Paula?"

I said it pointedly, glaring at Mum, trying to force her to speak.

She shook her head and mouthed the words *shut up* to me. Paula was smiling nervously, looking from Mum to me and back again. After a few moments' quiet she frowned, lines appearing on her forehead like train tracks.

"You know, Mum, about what happened to you. Twenty years ago?"

My voice was firm. If only she would tell it. If only she would open that box in her head and let it all come out.

"Is there something, Terri?" Paula said.

"No. . . Not really. . . What Stella means is that . . . I wanted to say how kind you've been. There was no one like you twenty years ago in Little Madden. That's all I wanted to say. Unless, Stella? You had something to add?"

Mum looked at me. Paula looked at me. She knew there was something more going on here.

"Well," I said, knowing then that I could never tell Mum's story for her. It would only be the right thing to do if she told it. "Well, just to say thanks for looking after us, in the flat, I mean."

A mobile phone sounded. Paula took it out of her bag and turned away from us.

"*Right . . . right . . . right now . . .*" she said and then turned back to us. "Things are developing. I'll have to go. I'm sure I'll see you around."

"Is it good news?" Mum said.

Paula didn't answer. She shook her head. Her lips were pursed tightly together. She turned and walked quickly up the hallway and out of the front door.

I looked at Mum.

"Is that it, Stel? Any more surprises for me?" she said, standing up, taking a deep breath, turning to the sink to refill her glass.

I didn't answer. I turned and walked out of the room.

THIRTY-TWO

I went out into the street. I figured I had done enough. I wasn't annoyed; I just felt frustrated. I had done nothing but listen to advice from adults over the last few years, especially Mum. Most of it I'd taken and even the stuff I had turned down, like staying on at school, I'd really thought hard about. But here was Mum, completely uninterested in what I had to say. And this time it wasn't about some stupid boyfriend; it was about something so huge, so momentous, that it made me feel nauseous just to think about it.

I plonked myself on our garden wall in front of the boards that covered our windows. I glared around, hoping to come face to face with one of the neighbours who had been so vile the previous week. There was no one, not even old Mrs Simpson, who was usually around somewhere.

Mum had made her up her mind years before. The fact that I knew didn't make any difference. She had lived with it for years and intended to go on in the same way. Had it affected her life? She had her job and the house and me. These were the solid things in her life. She'd never had a proper long-term relationship with a man. Was it because she didn't want to get involved with someone her own age, a real partner, someone who she might have to open up to? How could she open up to anyone while she was carrying this yoke around her neck?

I sighed.

A door opened further up and Raymond came out.

"Hi, kid!" he shouted.

I gave him a half-hearted wave. He was wearing his work clothes and he had a rolled-up newspaper under his arm. He went to his van and opened the back of it. I noticed, beyond him – parked further up the street, near the forest – the orange cable van. It was half up on the pavement and looked lopsided, as though it might tip over. The green sign *CommLink* stood out, garishly as ever. When were those people ever going to finish laying their cables?

Raymond appeared from behind his van holding a tape measure.

"I'll measure the window," he said when he got nearer. "I could pick up some glass today and fix it tonight when I get back from work."

I nodded, noticing, as he passed by, a strong scent coming off him; aftershave or maybe cologne. Poor Raymond. He wasn't the sort of man I'd expect to wear those things. He liked Mum, though. Trouble was, he just wasn't her type. She liked her men young and thin and preferably cold-hearted. I heard him singing, humming a tune happily. He was better off without my mum. Her problems were too complicated for him.

A siren sounded far away, in the distance. I glanced down the street towards the Hendersons'. Paula Bramble's car was parked there. She'd gone there straight from Mum. I felt a spurt of indignation thinking of this. I hoped she had made it perfectly clear that my mum had nothing to do with Jade's disappearance. Then I felt uncomfortable. Mrs Henderson had more important things to worry about than my mum's feelings.

A car turned into the street. It pulled up by Paula Bramble's and two men got out of it, slamming the doors with force, talking to each other rapidly, their words loud in the empty street. They were the police, I was sure. They disappeared into the Hendersons'. Further away I could hear another siren. Was it coming this way? I found myself sitting up on the wall, my back straight as a rod.

"Maybe they've found something," Raymond said, using a small pencil from behind his ear to write on a tiny pad.

A window opened above. It was Mum looking down from her bedroom. She gave me a tentative smile.

"Hey, Terri!" Raymond said. "Gonna sort this window out."

Mum nodded as the noise of the siren came closer and then stopped abruptly as a second car turned into the street. Its light was still flashing. I expected it to stop at the Hendersons', but it didn't. It moved slowly along, as though it was in no hurry at all, even though its light was blinking doggedly. As it passed us I could hear a voice from the radio inside talking urgently. It passed Raymond's van and the cable van and then came to a stop in the middle of the road, slanted so that no one could get by it. No one got out.

I stood up. I could feel something in the air, something electric.

"What's happening?" Mum called down.

I shook my head, my neck stretched so that I could see up the street. Behind me I could sense more people around, front doors opening and people coming out of their houses. Raymond moved out by his van as another police car came from the opposite direction, from the forest end of the street. It stopped in front of the slanted car and two uniformed officers got out immediately and ran towards the cable van. One of them stood at the back door and seemed to be looking in through the glass.

"Oh no," Raymond said. "No."

I didn't know what he meant, why he was saying it. His face had tightened, his lips pulled across his teeth.

"Raymond, what's happened?" Mum called.

The policeman had a hand at each side of his face so that he could better look into the window of the cable van. The other policeman went round other end and seemed to be doing the same there.

I can't see anything, one shouted.

The other police car started to reverse and did a swinging turn so that it faced down the street again. It revved past us. I watched it go to the end of the road and disappear. Then I saw the commotion outside the Hendersons'.

Paula Bramble was there, and the two plainclothes

men who'd got out of the car moments before. In the middle of them, in a blue dress, was Mrs Henderson. She was shouting, shrugging them off, moving up the street towards us. I looked fearfully up at Mum, remembering the night a week before when she had been aiming for our house. Mum seemed to shrink back from the window. I looked back and saw her marching, her arms at her sides, her hands in fists. Her face was rigid and the others were walking alongside her, their mouths and opening and closing. In moments she passed me without a glance or a look towards Mum. Her eyes were on the policeman, on the cable van and just at that moment I knew what was happening. It came to me suddenly. She thought, the policeman thought, that Jade Henderson was in that van. My legs went weak and I leaned back against the wall.

"Jade?" she shouted, walking off the pavement towards it, her big body getting further away from me, her dress hanging limp. Paula Bramble was talking constantly to her: *Cathy, this is not a good thing to do. This won't help anyone. You have to let us look after Jade now.*

Mrs Henderson's name was *Cathy*. I hadn't known, but instantly she seemed different to me, younger, less formidable.

The two policeman were waiting for her, standing across the back of the van. She stopped. I could only see her back but I expected her to start screaming at the top of her voice, the way she had when she came to our house. The policemen looked apprehensive; they had their arms out, as if expecting to control a crowd. Paula Bramble and the others were around Mrs Henderson. They were all talking to her, gesticulating with their hands, their voices criss-crossing each other. She was like a statue in the middle of them.

I could hear familiar sounds from behind me. Gloria was there and so was Mrs Simpson. There was mumbling from further away, the news spreading down the street. I heard the words *Body . . . cable van . . . arrested a man. . .* My mouth was dry and I looked up and saw Mum gripping the curtains, her eyes on Mrs Henderson.

There was a moment's silence and then Mrs Henderson's legs seemed to give way and she fell on her knees. I felt a collective gasp and moved forward, unable to drag my eyes away from her. Paula Bramble had squatted down and I heard someone behind me say something about an ambulance.

A thin cry went up, like a dog howling.

It was Mrs Henderson. No longer upright. Just a huddle of blue dress on the ground.

I looked round, up at Mum. Her face was white, her mouth twisted with anguish. She backed away and the window shut like a guillotine. I turned, my eyes drawn to the awful scene that was unfolding in the street in front of me.

THIRTY-THREE

It didn't take long for the street to fill up with police cars and journalists and sightseers, so I went indoors and stayed there. Mum's bedroom door was closed tightly all morning and I didn't knock or go in. I went into my room and sat at the back window looking out into the forest. The trees shimmered in the sun, the branches lifting and dropping in the warm breeze, the leaves flapping. It was tranquil. It looked like a picture on a postcard.

On the other side of the house was the lane and the cable van and the police. It was two different worlds.

About twelve I heard Mum's door open and shut and her footsteps down the stairs. She was moving about downstairs for a while. I didn't go out. I didn't know what to say to her. Then I thought I heard the front door open and shut. A while later the doorbell rang. I went downstairs sluggishly. It was Raymond.

"The police have found Jade Henderson's body," he said.

"In the cable van?" I said.

He shook his head.

"In the forest. One of the men who worked for the cable company made friends with her. His workmate found her toy monkey in his van. He went to the police."

"How terrible," I said.

Jade Henderson had been in the forest all the time.

Later I went to Mum's bedroom window and looked out on to the street. The cable van had been surrounded by white screens. There were policeman standing outside it. When I looked in the opposite direction I could see some neighbours, still out there, still looking, still gossiping.

I looked at the van again, some of it visible from the height of Mum's bedroom. It had been in the street for weeks. There were two or three men who worked from it, digging up the pavement and laying the cable. Afterwards they covered it up with uneven black tarmac that glittered in the sun as it hardened. Which one of those men took Jade Henderson and left her in the forest?

On Mum's desk I noticed my letter from the job agency. I picked it up. How inconsequential it was. How unimportant. Stay at school, get a job. What did any of these things matter when the world was full of fearful things? I went and sat on Mum's bed, pulling the duvet around my feet. I lay down and after a while I must have closed my eyes.

I opened them as Mum's room door opened. She was standing there dressed as if for work. She had one of her suits on and shoes and tights and looked stern. She was also carrying her briefcase.

"What?" I said, worried.

"I've just been to a solicitor," she said briskly. "He's meeting me at the police station in half an hour. You were right. This is too big for me to keep it to myself. It's not right. It's not fair. Lizzie is all grown up now and she'll have to deal with it in the best way she can. The truth has to come out. I'm going to see Paula Bramble and I'm going to tell her everything. She's expecting me."

I sat up. She came and sat on the bed beside me. I didn't know what to say to her. I was immediately anxious.

"What will the police do?"

"It doesn't matter what they do. It's time to tell it all. I've got the photos here," she said, pointing to her briefcase. "There's every chance that they might be able to find out something from them."

"Shall I come with you?" I said.

"Oh yes," she said, putting her arm around my shoulder, "you have to come. I need you there. I can't do this unless you're with me."

"Oh."

"I might be charged with withholding evidence. There's a chance I might go to prison. You have to be ready for that."

"Prison?" I said.

"It doesn't matter to me. It's got to come out. I can't carry this around with me any more. I've got to be strong. We've got to be strong. You get your stuff. Be quick. I've got a taxi picking us up at the high road in ten minutes."

I went into my room and picked my bag and my mobile up. My thoughts were racing. This was what I had wanted and yet now that it had come I felt slightly nauseous. *Prison.* What did that mean?

At the front door Mum paused and put her hand on my arm.

"The press will probably get hold of this. It might be bad, you know, with the neighbours. We might have all that attention again."

I nodded.

"They might be outside the door, shouting abuse. Like last time."

I nodded. My heart was racing at the thought of it.

"But this time I'm not running away," she said.

I followed her out into the street. We zigzagged along, past neighbours and journalists. All of them ignored us. We lowered our heads and walked in silence past the Hendersons' bungalow. At the bottom of our street we got into a waiting taxi.

We sat side by side and Mum held my hand tightly.

EPILOGUE

The sea is stunning here in Devon. The light reflects off it in so many ways. Early morning, midday, late at night. It's everything a photographer could want.

The cottage is perfect for us, on the edge of the village. We can keep ourselves to ourselves or we can take part in village life. People know me as Margaret Madden the wildlife photographer. They like us, we are popular, especially Jessica, my daughter.

We have a good life. Jessica is a beautiful young woman. She is accomplished. She plays the piano and the flute and she speaks three languages. She's just finished a degree in Classics and is working in one of the hotels for the summer. She doesn't need to work as I have a good income but she likes to do the things her friends do and I understand that.

I love her. She is everything to me. I don't regret a single thing I did.

Sometimes I look in the mirror and I say, Margaret Madden, you are the luckiest woman alive.

No one will find us. I will never let it happen.

The End